Frankie's Run

Frankie's Run
Mary C. Ryan

Little, Brown and Company
Boston   Toronto

First Edition

Library of Congress Cataloging-in-Publication Data
Ryan, Mary C.
  Frankie's run.

  Summary: As she and her best friend really start to
grow up and enter the boy-watching stage, thirteen-year-
old Mary Frances wonders if she should try to be like
everyone else or fight for her own identity.
  [1. Identity — Fiction] I. Title.
PZ7.R9545Fr 1987   [Fic]   86-20114
ISBN 0-316-76370-5

RRD-VA

Designed by Trisha Hanlon

Published simultaneously in Canada
by Little, Brown & Company (Canada) Limited

Printed in the United States of America

To all those who believed,
my deepest thanks.

Frankie's Run

Chapter 1

It sure is funny how a bunch of completely unrelated things can come together all of a sudden and change a person's whole life. When I mentioned this to my mother, she said it was a Very Profound Thought. If it was, I hope I never have another one. My head is tired of having so much stuff running around inside it.

Looking back over the past few months, though, it's entirely possible that if Jason Kirchfield had lived in Antarctica, and if Kicky didn't love Walt Disney movies, and if gum would stick where it's supposed to, and a whole string of other "ifs," I probably would have stayed just plain old Mary Frances Courtney, instead of becoming a celebrity.

In a way, it was like one of those Saturday morning cartoons. There's this mouse who's trying to get away from the big, bad cat, so he makes a little snowball and starts rolling it down the hill. On the way, it keeps picking up more and more snow until it gets really enormous and there's this poor unsuspecting cat standing at the bottom. POW!

I was the cat. I never saw it coming. So when Jeanine called me that Friday back in May and asked if I'd go to the Castello di Pizza with her for a while, I had no idea that disaster was headed my way.

Jeanine Tobin is my best friend. We met the first day of kindergarten. She and I happened to be the only ones not crying, so we just naturally started playing together and have been friends ever since. Now we're both thirteen and in the eighth grade at North Valley Junior High.

We don't look much alike, Jeanine and I. She has gorgeous long blonde hair, which she keeps looking superb with the help of about a thousand dollars' worth of electrical equipment. I inherited my father's red hair, although his is strawberry and mine is more carrot. It has all these little kinks in it, too. If I didn't keep it pulled back in a ponytail, it would look like a dust mop.

Jeanine has one of those complexions like the skin of a perfectly ripe peach. No self-respecting zit would be caught dead on it. Mine is paler, with red splotches here and there, especially when I blush. I also have freckles, which makes me look like I've been sprinkled with pepper.

I'm quite a bit taller than Jeanine, but I look sort of like the beanpole everyone mentions when they describe somebody who's skinny.

Despite our physical differences, though, Jeanine and I get along, except on those rare occasions when she wants to do something and I don't. Like just then, going to the Castello.

"*Now?*" I yelled into the phone. "I just finished eating!" That was an understatement. What I'd just finished was one of my mom's famous spaghetti dinners. As usual, I'd made a pig of myself.

"Oh, come on," Jeanine begged. "We don't have to eat anything. Just have a soda or something."

"Fat chance," I said. "You know how waitresses love teenagers sitting around without ordering."

"Then I'll get a pizza."

I began to get suspicious. Jeanine watched her weight the way a mother cat watched her kittens. She'd been known to diet for a week after eating one candy bar. There had to be some reason for her to sacrifice her waistline.

"Who's going to be there?" I asked casually.

There was a small silence. "Just the usual bunch, I suppose," she replied.

The light was finally dawning. "The usual bunch

wouldn't include Jason Kirchfield, would it?"

"He might drop in."

"Terrific."

My lack of enthusiasm was understandable. There's a Jason Kirchfield in every school. He was the quarterback of the ninth grade football team, the captain of the basketball team, pitched for the baseball team, and was probably the closest thing to God on the face of the earth from the tales I'd heard. And he knew it. He walked through the halls with his nose up in the air, a stupid grin on his face, and his chest so puffed up, you'd think one of his footballs was permanently stuck inside it. It beats me why girls always fall for that type, but they do.

Jeanine was his latest casualty. Every time she passed his locker, she'd touch the door and sigh. J's were scribbled all over her notebook covers. One day he actually said hello to her and she floated about ten feet off the ground for the rest of the afternoon. I felt like the Goodyear blimp was following me around.

"Please, Mary Frances?" she was saying over the phone now. "Please, please, please? Pretty please?"

I really didn't want to go. I can't stand watching people torture themselves. Jeanine had about as much chance of capturing Jason Kirchfield as I did of getting an *A* in science. Practically zilch.

"But I was going to watch a Jacques Cousteau special on TV tonight," I protested.

"Mary Frances, I saw the listings. It's going to be about seaweed. You hate seaweed, remember?"

She had me there. "Well, I hear we could be eating it one of these days. It might be a good idea to find out what it's like."

"It's slimy, Mary Frances. Green and slimy and full of all those little creatures . . ."

My stomach flopped. "That's enough, Jeanine. I'll go."

"You will? Do you mean it? You honestly will?"

"Isn't that what I just said?"

"Just making sure. I've got to go and get ready. Pick me up about quarter to eight, OK?"

As I hung up, I glanced at the hall clock. It was just six-thirty. Jeanine had enough time to get ready for a three-month African safari. Although a hunt was exactly what she had in mind, I guess.

Just then, the front door opened and my father, Timothy Daniel Courtney, walked in. A suitcase was in one hand and he had his briefcase tucked under his arm. He'd been away almost all week on a business trip for his company, Tower and Son Pharmaceuticals. He sells medical stuff to hospitals and doctors. Carolyn Kinkead asked me once if he was a drug pusher. I hate stupid kids.

"If it isn't my favorite redhead," he said, giving me a peck on the cheek before setting down his suitcase.

"Hi, Dad. How was the trip?"

"Long." He looked tired. His eyes almost matched his hair.

"I bet a plate of Mom's spaghetti will fix you up," I said. "Want me to fix you some?"

My mother is Jane Martin Courtney, Martin being her name before she married my father. Her family used to be Italian before her grandfather got tired of writing out "Martinelli" and had it shortened. That's probably why she makes such terrific spaghetti, though. We've practically lived on it for the past year — ever since she started working for Dr. Ralph Blessing, our dentist. (We all get our teeth fixed for half price.) She said she took the job because trying to feed our family was like the miracle of the loaves and fishes. Her working made life at home pretty hectic at first. The Apostles kicked up a big fuss about having to do dishes until my mother explained things to them. She has short dark hair with little sprinkles of gray in it when she forgets to color it.

At the mention of food, my father perked up a bit, but then he said he'd rather relax for a while first. "School go all right this week?" he asked.

"Fine," I mumbled, not particularly wanting to get into a conversation on that subject just then. I mean, it's nice that he's so interested and all, but I was afraid he might get around to my science grades. "As a matter of fact," I put in quickly, "I was just going to do some homework."

He gave me a big smile. "Well, don't let me keep you, sweetie. I'll wander into the kitchen and see what your mother's up to."

I breathed a sigh of relief. I hadn't lied about the homework. Mrs. Novelli, my science teacher, had given us an assignment for over the weekend. It was a real winner. We were supposed to write a five-hundred-word essay on a woman scientist. Everybody in the class decided right away that they'd do Marie Curie, because she was so well known for her discovery of radium. Lately, my science grade had sunk so low I could have used a team of scuba divers to bring them up. So, I thought if I chose someone else, Mrs. Novelli would be impressed and give me a higher mark. It was worth a try, and I had an hour to kill before meeting Jeanine. The only thing was, I didn't even know if there *were* any other women scientists.

Kicky was coming down the stairs as I headed up to my room.

"Hey, Mary Frances, want to watch Jacques Cousteau with me tonight?" He asked, his little face all excited. Kicky is never going to flunk science. I can tell that already.

"I'm afraid not, Kick," I said, giving his hair a mussing. "I'm going out. Anyway, it's about seaweed. Green, slimy, full of little creatures . . ."

"Yeah!" he crowed. "Won't it be great?"

Kicky (his real name is Kevin) is the youngest in our family, which is a large one — enormous, in fact, compared to anyone else's these days. Altogether, we have eight people.

Kicky is six. When he was a baby, we all took turns feeding him and he'd just lie there in our laps, kicking his right foot like crazy while he slurped his milk. The name just kind of stuck. Once in a while I have to babysit him, and that was part of my snowball.

While Kicky went downstairs to convince my parents that they were really going to love seaweed, I continued up to my room. Angela was sitting on her bed painting her fingernails, probably for the fourth time that day. She puts on about three coats at once and then spends the next hour biting them off.

Angela is sixteen — three years older than me. She's the only one who inherited the Italian side of the family. She has long, almost-black hair, and real dark eyes. The Apostles used to tease her about being adopted until she started believing it and nearly ended up having to see a shrink.

The Apostles, by the way, are my brothers Matthew, Mark, and John. Matt and Mark are identical twins and are twenty years old. John is a year younger. They almost look like triplets, though — blond and stocky and all three of them growing beards and moustaches.

When John was baptized, Father Muhlbauer made some remark about their names sounding like the Apostles in the gospels. Pretty soon everybody lumped them under the one name. Since they do practically everything together, it makes it a lot easier. A lot of people assumed Kevin was just naturally going to be named Luke — to finish out the Apostles. My mother says she would have called him Banana Split first.

I ignored Angela and her eternal search for the perfect nail color and went right to my desk. Angela used to be a lot of fun when we were younger. Lately, though, she'd been a real pain. All she ever thought about was her hair and clothes. Oh, and boys, of course. My father says if he'd known he was going to have two daughters, he'd have built an extra bathroom in the house. Well, I only use it for what's necessary, so it's evident who spends most of her time in there.

The worst thing about Angela, though, is that she seems to think she owns me. She's full of advice about how I should do my hair and thinks it's terrible that I wear jeans all the time. My mother says I shouldn't pay any attention to it because Angela is "emerging," whatever that means. It makes me think of grubs coming out of the lawn. My mother also doesn't have to share her room with Angela.

I flipped open my science book. There was a whole chapter on Albert Einstein and his theory of something-or-other, and plenty about the Curies, naturally. As far as other women scientists were concerned, you'd have thought everything else in the world was discovered by a man. Still, I knew that Mrs. Novelli would never have given the assignment if the information wasn't available someplace. There was only one answer. I slammed the book shut and groaned.

"Homework on a Friday night?" Angela was waving her hands around like she was chasing flies.

"It's this stupid science paper," I said disgustedly. "I just realized I'm going to have to spend the entire day tomorrow at the library."

Angela stopped in mid shoo. "The library?"

I started rummaging around in my dresser for a clean sweatshirt. "I have a seventy-two average in science," I muttered, hauling out a navy blue one with GO FLY A KITE/KITTY HAWK printed across the front. "Dad will personally kill me if I don't bring it up. Therefore, I'm going to have to do a spectacular job of this assignment, just to show Novelli that I'm interested in getting a good grade."

Angela grinned from pierced ear to pierced ear. "How very clever of you, Mary Frances! You must have inherited all the brains in the family."

"Having a seventy-two average is brainy?"

"Of course not. It's just that you're so — so clever."

For someone who's usually lost in her own little world, Angela's taking an interest in my brain was definitely abnormal. In fact, this was the first time she'd ever openly admitted that I even had one. It suddenly occurred to me that this was the second time in less than an hour that I had to try and figure out the real reason somebody wanted me to do something. I wish people would come out and say what they mean. Life would be a lot simpler.

I waited. Angela would get to the point sooner or later. It didn't take long.

"Bill Warnock asked me if I'd drive out to the airport with him tomorrow to pick up his father," she went on.

"So?"

"So, it's my turn to take Kicky to the library to see the Walt Disney movie."

"And you want me to take him."

"You just said you were going there."

I sighed. "I took him last time, remember?"

Kicky, I should mention, is a Walt Disney freak. I bet he's seen every movie the man ever made at least once, and some probably five times. For the past few months, the library had been running a special Saturday program of Disney films. Kicky hadn't missed one.

"I'll pay you back," Angela promised earnestly. "It's just that I think Bill is going to ask me to the Junior Prom and the sooner I know if he is, the sooner I can start planning what to wear."

That could have taken until next November. I sighed again. "All right, Angela. But you owe me one."

"You're a doll, Mary Frances!"

I was a doll, all right. A puppet was more like it. People kept pulling strings and I kept hopping around. I yanked the sweatshirt over my head, gave my ponytail a few quick swipes with a brush, and headed out the door to call Jeanine. As I left, Angela started biting off her nail polish.

Chapter 2

It was still a little early when Jeanine and I got to the Castello. Hardly anybody ever showed up before eight-thirty, but Jeanine had said she wanted to get there before the crowd. Which meant, it turned out, that she wanted to make sure she got a seat with a good view of the door. So she'd know the instant Jason Kirchfield put the toe of his sneaker inside the place.

My view was of a baby in a high chair at the end of the booth next to ours. The chair had a bright yellow balloon tied on it, and the baby was more interested in that than in the squares of pizza that littered his tray. Every once in a while he'd pick up one of the squares, but before he could get it to his mouth, the balloon would catch his attention again, and the pizza generally ended up in his ear. Actually, it was pretty funny. A lot better than watching a door.

The Castello is the local hangout, although families go there, too. It's decorated in typical pizza-parlor style — lots of dark wood and red and white checkerboard tablecloths with little red hurricane lamps so you can see what you're eating. Up near the cash register were a couple of video games.

Right after we sat down, the waitress appeared and wanted to know if we were ready to order. Jeanine said she needed a couple of minutes to look over the menu, as if she was going to order a six-course dinner or something.

"We don't want to get our pizza too soon," she explained after the waitress had gone. She unzipped her jacket and slipped it off. "Jason probably won't show up for a while."

I stared at her in amazement — not because of what she'd said, but because of what she was wearing.

I had on my GO FLY A KITE sweatshirt. That's the way I normally dress, and Jeanine, up until now, had done the same. My father often joked about having two sets of twins, Jeanine being over at our house so much and all. Well, Jeanine now had on a pink plaid blouse with a soft pink sweater over the top. She looked, to tell the truth, just like one of those cutesy Valentine cards.

"New sweater?" I asked, folding my arms across my chest to hide my sweatshirt.

"Do you like it? My mom and I dashed out to the store after school."

"Boy, you're really going all out," I remarked dryly. "I hope Jason appreciates the effort."

She blushed — pinkly. "It's not just for Jason. I got tired of bumming around in sloppy clothes."

She really knew how to make a person feel good.

The waitress returned. She was definitely miffed when I said I'd just have a soda, but brightened considerably with Jeanine's order of a small cheese with pepperoni and mushrooms. I hate mushrooms. They remind me of seaweed.

Suddenly Jeanine said, "Change places with me, Mary Frances. I don't want Jason to see me when he comes in."

"I thought that's what we're here for," I said.

"We are, but I don't want him to know that."

Maybe it made sense. To Jeanine, anyway. Besides, the baby was getting boring. I moved.

The Castello was beginning to fill up. Most of the booths were taken, and the video games were doing a brisk business. I waved at a couple of kids from school.

"Who's that?" Jeanine demanded.

"Patti Hodgeson. Relax, Jeanine. I'll let you know."

Our drinks came. Jeanine checked her reflection in

her glass and pulled out her comb to put a few stray locks back in place. Then she shook her hair back and forth across her shoulders like in the shampoo commercials. I wished I could do that.

After about twenty minutes, the pizza had appeared, but not Jason Kirchfield. Jeanine was beginning to fidget. Every three seconds she asked, "Is he here yet?" until I began to understand how my parents felt when we went on a long car trip.

The spaghetti had long worn off, as spaghetti tends to do. I downed two slices of pizza (no mushrooms), but Jeanine seemed to have lost her appetite.

I was just pulling a third slice off the pan, wrapping the cheese around my finger so it wouldn't slop all over my clothes, when the Castello door opened and Jason Kirchfield swaggered into the place. That's the only way I can describe it. He still wore that silly grin on his face, and his varsity jacket was opened all the way down, allowing his chest to stick out like a hot dog in a bun.

"Your prayers have been answered," I whispered to Jeanine.

Immediately she ducked down in the booth. "You mean it? What's he wearing?"

"Clothes."

She ignored that. "Who's with him?"

"A bunch of guys."

She heaved a sigh of relief and ventured a peek

around the corner. Fortunately (or unfortunately — you never know with Jeanine), Jason wasn't looking.

I watched with her. Jason was talking to some kids at the video games. Next to him was a boy I'd never seen before. I was looking at his back, but I could tell he was somebody new. Riding a school bus had trained me to recognize people from behind. He was slightly shorter than Jason and had light, straw-colored hair. I wondered who he was.

Jeanine saw him, too. "Who's that?" she asked.

"I don't know," I said.

Then he turned. "He has a nice nose," murmured Jeanine, as if such things were important. I personally considered noses about the same as knees. Necessary, but not exactly beautiful. I had to admit that Jeanine was right this time, though. Whoever he was, he did have a nice nose. It began and ended just where you'd want it to, with no detours in between.

Jason Kirchfield decided to do an about-face, also, sending Jeanine flying back to safety.

"It's too late," I warned her. "Hold your breath, Jeanine. He's coming over."

I waited for her to faint. She surprised me, though. Within two seconds, she was as cool as a Popsicle.

"Well, hello, Jason," she said in a deep, sexy voice that reminded me a bit of Jane Fonda, but not particularly Jeanine Tobin.

His chest inflated ever farther, if that was possible.

"Hello, yourself. Mind if we join you?" He motioned to the boy with the nice nose, who was standing beside him.

I knew Jeanine was dying of joy, but she just smiled and moved over on the seat. My opinion obviously wasn't needed, but I moved, too, and let the boy slip in next to me.

Jason and Jeanine sat there grinning at each other until it began to get downright embarrassing. I mean, after all, hadn't Jason ever heard of making an introduction? I cleared my throat, hoping somebody would notice. When nothing happened, I ventured a sharp kick at Jeanine's ankle. I must have missed. Jason sat up suddenly and glared across the table. But it did the trick.

"Uh, this is Jeanine and — er—"

"Mary Frances," I helped.

"Oh, yeah. This is Bruce Herrman. He just moved in on our street."

"Two r's," said Bruce Herrman.

"What has two r's?" I asked.

He smiled. I could see he had nice, straight teeth. Like his nose. "Herrman," he said. "Brrrruce would sound like I was freezing to death."

I looked at Bruce "Two r's" Herrman with interest. The guy actually had a sense of humor. He might have been new in town, but he sure wasn't shy. He was nice. "Hi," I said.

"Hi."

Jeanine and Jason had returned to playing Romeo and Juliet. I glanced at Bruce and shrugged. He nodded, as if to say, "I know what you mean."

"Want to try out a video game?" he asked after a few more minutes of deadly quiet.

There wasn't much sense sitting there with two blocks of wood, so I said OK, first checking to make sure I had a couple of extra quarters in my pocket. It turned out not to matter, though, because he paid for both games of "1812," where you sailed two ships around in the water and fired cannonballs at the other guy. It was pretty generous of him, considering the fact that I beat him twice. I explained that I'd learned the game on a home set that belonged to a friend of my brothers. He said it was fun anyway and we got to talking about school (he was in the eighth grade, too), where he came from (Oklahoma), and how the Yankees would do this year (probably take the Series). He was easy to talk to.

When we finally went back to the booth, the one last slice of pizza had dried up, the pepperoni hardened into an orange pool of grease. I won't even describe the mushrooms, except that they were a lot livelier than the two eye-wrestling contestants. After a couple of minutes, Jeanine looked up. "Hey, you two don't have to sit here all the time," she said. "Why don't you go play a video game or something?" Bruce buried his face in his hands.

Suddenly, Jason glanced at his watch and jumped

up. "Gosh, it's almost nine-thirty. I have to get up early for ball practice. Let's go, Bruce. See you later, Jeanine. You, too, — uh—"

"Gretchen," I supplied. He was still trying to figure it out when he left. Bruce Herrman was laughing.

Jeanine and I left a short time later. I'd had the waitress wrap up the rest of the pizza so Kicky could have it for breakfast the next morning.

Outside, Jeanine still seemed lost in another world. "He's going to the dance next Friday," she said, all dreamylike, as we walked down the sidewalk. "He said he'd meet me there."

"Why doesn't he just take you?" I asked.

She flashed me a look of sheer exasperation. "It doesn't work that way, Mary Frances." I don't know. It sounded like she was trying to convince herself. "And how about Bruce?" she asked then, slyly.

"What about Bruce?"

"You can't fool me, Mary Frances. I saw you two talking to each other."

That was doubtful. But I asked, "What's that supposed to mean?"

"He likes you."

"I like him."

Jeanine grabbed my arm. "Oh, won't it be neat? We can double-date!"

"Whoa, Jeanine." I stopped in my tracks. "I said I like him. I don't looove him, like you looove Jason. He's a nice guy. Now forget it."

But Jeanine was like a dog with a bone. "It'll be so great, the four of us. Wait until we fix you up. New hairstyle, maybe a little eye shadow . . ." She was a half block away, still muttering to herself, before she realized I hadn't budged a step. "What's the matter?" she cried, running back.

"You're starting to sound just like Angela, that's what's the matter. We are *not* fixing me up, Jeanine. First, because there's no reason to, and second, because I'd rather not look like some creature out of a horror show, thank you."

Jeanine gets pretty good grades in school, but sometimes it takes a bulldozer to get things through her head. She hopped along beside me saying, ". . . but . . . but . . . but . . . ," and sounding like a motorboat. With luck, she'd finally run out of gas.

Just then I heard footsteps running along behind us. I stepped off onto the grass and dragged Jeanine with me, still sputtering.

"Well, look who's out doing the town," said a voice out of the darkness. I peered closer. It was my brother Matt, dressed in shorts and a T-shirt, jogging in place on the walk. The moon lit up streaks of sweat dripping off his beard.

"Hi, Matt. The girls after you again?"

"No, dear lady — *ladies*," he corrected with a nod at Jeanine. "I'll have you know I'm in training."

"Funny way to train for drinking beer," I commented. "Is this supposed to make you more thirsty?"

Chapter 3

Needless to say, I was not terribly bright and cheery the next day. Not only hadn't I gotten much sleep, but over my head was still hanging the evil shadow of Mrs. Novelli's assignment. The last thing I felt like doing was rooting through dusty shelves of books in the library. But the paper had to be done, regardless of how I felt, and anyway, I had promised Angela I'd take Kicky to the movie.

We left shortly after lunch. Kicky chirped along the whole eight blocks, skipping and pointing out neat things like a three-legged dog and a chalked hopscotch on the sidewalk, which he insisted we play on for a while until I reminded him about the time. It was a beautiful spring day, and the sunshine did a lot for my grouchiness. By the time we got to the library, I felt more like tackling the job.

As soon as we got in the door, Kicky took off with a whole bunch of other screaming kids into the Children's Room. I went over to the reference section and asked the librarian if she could help me find some information on female scientists.

"Is this for school?" she asked. "We've had two other requests for that particular topic today."

I nodded, hoping she'd given them books on Marie Curie.

As if in answer to my prayer, she said, "There's a great deal of information on Marie Curie, of course."

"I have to do somebody else."

"Oh. Well, I'll see what I can do."

She was gone a long time. I busied myself sharpening the pencils I'd brought. Finally she returned with one volume of an encyclopedia in her hand. "Maybe in a few years, we'll have a bit more representation in the scientific field," she commented with a woman-to-woman smile. She handed me the book, pointing to a heading: "Florence Rena Sabin." I'd never heard of her. "This was all I could find just now," said the librarian, apologetically. "It's rather short."

I'll say it was short. Florence Rena Sabin was born in Colorado and studied cells, the bloodstream, and tuberculosis. It didn't seem like much to describe a whole life's work. Even with adding a bunch of my own words, I only ended up with both sides of one page — and most of that was scratched-out words.

At a quarter to three, I wandered out to the front desk because another thing Kicky likes to do is get lost. Once he really did. The police took him to the station house and fed him chocolate ice cream cones. My father had a hard time prying him loose. Ever since, if he even thinks nobody's around, he starts yelling bloody murder in the hope that the cops will come and get him again.

The door to the Children's Room was still shut. I strolled around looking at all the brochures that were set out for people to take. At a nearby bulletin board, a man was pinning up a notice. There wasn't anything else of interest to do, so I walked over and stood behind him, reading over his shoulder. It took a minute or two for the words on the paper to sink in. When they did, I gasped out loud.

The man spun around, startled. I'd probably scared him half to death. He had a pleasant face, sort of round, and he wore heavy black glasses that made him look slightly like an owl, except that an owl has feathers, whereas he was almost completely bald. A badge on the lapel of his sport coat read "James Muldoon, Library Director."

"May I be of some assistance?" he asked politely when he recovered.

"That notice," I said, pointing to it. "It says the

Walt Disney movies are going to be canceled. Is that true?"

He ran his fingers through what was left of his hair. "I'm afraid so, young lady. Today will be the final one."

"That's terrible!" I cried, thinking about Kicky and how disappointed he was going to be. "I mean—" I hesitated, not quite sure of what else to say. "But why?"

"Financial difficulties. Frankly, we just can't afford to run these free programs any longer."

In my mind I could imagine all the other kids like Kicky who were going to be pretty sad when next Saturday rolled around. "Do they have to be free?" I asked Mr. Muldoon. "Couldn't you just charge a dollar or something? It would still be a lot cheaper than a regular show."

He shook his head. "The Disney studio has strict regulations which prohibit charging admission for the films when they're used by educational institutions."

"Oh." I turned away. It didn't seem fair somehow. But our school had just cut some programs for the same reason, so I supposed the library wasn't the only place that had money problems.

Just then the movie let out. From the excited looks on the kids' faces, it was pretty evident that the library staff hadn't had the heart to tell them about the cancellation. They were leaving it up to the parents.

I plowed through the crowd to find Kicky before he could start yelling. I caught him just in time. He was looking hopeful. In fact, his mouth was half open.

"How was the movie, Kick?" I asked, fast.

The yell got swallowed and his face lit up like it always does when he thinks about Walt Disney. "Gee, Mary Frances, you should have *seed* it!" he squeaked. "There was these orphan kids and they went to live . . ."

I stopped him before he could inform the whole library. "We have to be outside right away, unless you feel like walking home. The Apostles are supposed to pick us up. They won't like it if we're late."

As I predicted, Mark had his foot on the gas pedal of our old green station wagon, revving the motor like he was at the Indy 500. I shoved Kicky into the back and just about got the door closed before Mark peeled off.

"Take it easy!" I yelled. "I almost lost my head!"

"That might be an improvement," remarked Matt, nudging John.

"You should have seed that movie," Kicky began again. "There was these kids . . ."

"*Seen*," I corrected, but this time he kept going.

". . . and they were orphans and they went to live with this lady and she was learning to be a witch and she had this bedknob . . ."

"What's a bedknob?" asked John, pretending he didn't know. Maybe he didn't.

"It's some kind of round thing off a bed, and . . ."

"I have one," I put in.

Kicky's eyes bulged. "Do you really, Mary Frances? Gee, do you think I could borrow it when we get home? The one in the movie made the bed fly all over the place."

"I don't think mine does that."

He never heard me. "I could go to the North Pole and see Santa Claus," he was crooning to himself.

Mark swerved to avoid hitting a dog. "You wouldn't want to go there, Kick. You'd spoil all the fun of seeing what you got on Christmas morning."

Kicky's chin jutted out. "Well, I'll go someplace else, then."

"Lotsa luck," I murmured. Secretly, though, I hoped he could get the thing working. It would be a good way of escaping some of Angela's lectures.

As soon as we got home, Kicky went to pour out the whole story to my father, who was mowing the lawn. I went up to my room. Angela was doing more emerging — this time from the bathroom. It's a wonder she hadn't worn a path in the hall carpet yet.

"You'll be happy to learn that after today, you can go riding anywhere you like with Bill Warnock on Saturdays," I told her. "The library had to cut out the Disney movies. No money."

To be perfectly honest, Angela really does have some nice qualities. She has a real soft spot in her heart for Kicky. She reads him stories and once went to his open house at school when our parents were out of town. "That's awful!" she cried. "The poor kid's going to be heartbroken. Does he know yet?"

I shook my head. "I couldn't say anything. He was so excited about — *whooops*, I forgot." I yanked the wooden ball off my headboard and went across the hall.

Kicky was changing into his play clothes. When he saw the bedknob, he was so delighted he threw his polo shirt on backward and snatched it out of my hand. Then he plopped down on his bed and closed his eyes. I guess he was going to try a quick trip to the North Pole, after all. I left him there, his face all scrunched up and the bedknob clutched tightly in his fist.

My science paper didn't turn out too badly. I threw in a lot of stuff about the need for more women going into science, mentioned Marie Curie and her daughter a couple of times, and put a cover on it with test tubes that had little aprons tied around their middles. If nothing else, it at least looked like I'd put some effort into it. Which I had.

Supper was ready at about five o'clock. The Apostles had been hovering over the oven for the past half hour, so my mother sent me to call Kicky and Angela.

Kicky was still sitting on his bed holding the bedknob. "It doesn't work, Mary Frances," he sobbed, tears trickling down his face.

It didn't exactly seem like the right time to tell him

about the Disney movies. "I'm kind of glad it didn't, Kick," I said, giving him a hug. "I like having you around."

"Aw, I wasn't going far. Just down to the store." He opened his fist. Resting on his palm was one grubby nickle.

"Tell you what — shut your eyes real tight. Don't peek! Now, *abracadabra* . . ." I lifted him up and whisked him down the stairs into the dining room. "Presto!"

He giggled. "That was neat, Mary Frances! Do it again!"

Since I'd almost dropped him the first time, I thought I'd better leave well enough alone. "Some other time. Supper's ready."

Angela and I are supposed to do the dishes together on Saturdays, but that night I ended up doing most of the work. Good old Warnock had come through and asked her to the Junior Prom. She was on Cloud Nine. She'd take one plate off the table, then dance to the dishwasher with it, humming some kind of waltzy tune. I couldn't see what she was so excited about. I mean, a dance is a dance, regardless of what you call it.

I was just mopping up the counters when the door-bell rang. I went to answer it and found Jeanine on the porch, her eyes dripping wet and her hair, for once, a mess.

"That two-timer!" she wailed at me even before I had a chance to ask what was the matter. "That rotten, no-good . . ."

Question answered. "Jason Kirchfield," I said.

"Jason *Rotten* Kirchfield, you mean!" She stomped into the house, down the hall and into the kitchen, where she flung herself into a chair. I followed along behind. I took a glass from the cupboard and filled it with some lemonade. If anybody ever needed a drink, it was Jeanine.

By this time, Angela had finally stopped her humming and was staring dreamily out the window. She glanced over as Jeanine let out a loud sniff.

"Golly, you look *terrible!*" she cried.

"That's because I *feel* terrible!" Jeanine exclaimed. "Terribly, horribly —" Words failed her. "— mad," she finished lamely. She sipped the lemonade. Angela and I waited. "I went over to the ball field to watch Jason practice this morning," she sputtered at last. "I hid behind the bleachers, though. I didn't want him to know I was there." Typical Jeanine logic. "Then, who shows up but Sarah Proefrock with a bunch of her stupid friends and they start talking to him. They were all crowding around him like he was an ice cream truck. Then, Sarah said . . . She said . . ."

"*What did she say?*" Angela and I screamed together, unable to stand the suspense.

Jeanine took a deep breath and went on. Or tried to. "She said . . ." Her voice rose to a squeaky-high pitch. "She said, 'Jason, could you save me just one little dance next Friday?' Oh, it was *sickening*. You should have been there."

I was awfully glad I wasn't.

"So, what did Jason say?" Angela urged.

Here Jeanine almost broke down altogether. "He said . . ." She blew her nose on a paper napkin. "He said, 'How about every other one?' "

"The rat!" growled Angela.

"Calm down, Jeanine," I said reasonably. "That leaves you with all the rest, doesn't it? Fifty-fifty isn't such a bad deal."

She just stared at me, speechless.

Angela went over and put her arm around Jeanine. "Just forget about him," she advised in a motherly tone. "There are other fish in the sea. Mary Frances doesn't understand." She flashed me a look, then added mysteriously, "Yet."

Jeanine sniffed. "But I don't want any other fish. It's all right for Mary Frances to be so casual about it. She still has Bruce."

"*Bruce?*" Angela's ears quivered like antennas.

"Shut up, Jeanine," I snapped. "I don't 'have' anybody. What's more, I don't 'want' anybody."

"Who's Bruce?"

"Never mind, Angela."

"Bruce is this really neat new guy we met last night at the Castello," Jeanine babbled. "He and Mary Frances got along just super. He really likes her. He *does*, Mary Frances," she insisted when I opened my mouth to protest. "You're blind not to see it."

"I am not blind. You have an overactive imagination."

Angela was trying to recover from the shock. "Mary Frances has a boyfriend?" she breathed in awe. "I don't believe it!"

"That's fine, Angela," I said. "Keep right on not believing it. It happens not to be true, anyway." I glared at Jeanine to keep her from opening her mouth any farther.

"Then why are you blushing?" Angela asked with a smirk.

I put my hand to my cheek. It *was* warm. I probably had red splotches from my forehead to my Adam's apple. "Anyone would be embarrassed the way you two are carrying on!" I yelled.

"Sure, Mary Frances." She and Jeanine exchanged looks. It occurred to me that Jeanine was recovering from her trauma in record time.

As coolly as I could, I said, "If you two want to sit here all night and discuss my life, be my guests. I have to read a chapter for social studies." I stomped out of the kitchen, leaving them in a fit of giggles behind me.

Upstairs, I flopped on my bed. Why couldn't people just leave me alone? It was bad enough that Angela was always trying to change me. Now Jeanine was doing it. It all seemed stupid and silly. Boys were just members of the human race, the same as girls. What was so great about them that people had to lose their senses? You wouldn't have caught Marie Curie — or Florence Rena Sabin, for that matter — going into hysterics because some guy wouldn't give them the time of day! They contributed something useful to the world. They'd found something better than eye shadow and pink sweaters to think about.

If I'd had a crystal ball at that moment, I would have seen a gigantic snowball, as big as a house, hanging over my head. And it was getting ready to drop.

Chapter 4

I woke up Monday morning to find my head stuck to my pillow. I must have yelped because Angela, who was in front of the mirror putting on eyeliner, spun around so fast that she drew a black line right across her face.

"Knock it off, Mary Frances!" she cried. "I'm not in the mood to play games."

"It's not a game, Angela. I can't get the pillow off. Honest!" I waggled my head. The pillow flopped merrily along.

With a sigh of exasperation, perfected through years of practice, she got up. "It's gum," she announced after a brief examination. "It's plastered all over. Don't you know enough to take it out before you go to sleep?"

"It's not mine!" I wailed. "I don't know where it came from. Please, Angela. You've got to help. I can't go to school like this."

A zillion hairs came out by the roots, but at last she managed to get the pillow free. However, I was still left with an enormous tangle at the back of my head. I could tell it was bad just from the look on Angela's face.

"Let me try some nail polish remover." She poured about half a bottle on the snarl, then scrubbed at it until my scalp stung. After about five minutes of this kind of torture, she finally gave up. "I'm going to miss my bus," she said. "You'd better see what Mom can do."

I put on my bathrobe and ran downstairs, reminding myself to stay away from the stove. What with all the nail polish remover fumes coming off my head, I could easily turn into a blazing bonfire.

My mother was sympathetic, but she didn't have any better luck. "I'm afraid there's only one solution," she said. "I'll get the scissors."

"Scissors! You can't cut all my hair off! I'll be bald!"

"Nonsense. I'll just snip off the snarl. You'll hardly notice it."

"If I keep my back to the wall all day," I muttered under my breath.

While she went to get the scissors, I glanced across the table at Kicky. He was shoveling cornflakes into his mouth faster than he could possibly swallow and not paying attention to me at all. He was definitely not his usual self. Then it struck me.

"Kicky."

No answer.

"Kicky, you didn't happen to put my bedknob back on my bed, did you?"

Another spoonful. He was beginning to look like a chipmunk.

"And it didn't happen to have your gum on it, did it?"

He swallowed, took a slug of orange juice, and croaked, "I'm awfully sorry, Mary Frances! I didn't mean it." I almost believed him until he added sourly, "The dumb thing didn't even work."

As if it was my fault that he hadn't ended up at the North Pole. At that point, it wouldn't have been such a bad idea. But the damage was done. There wasn't much use in staying mad at him. I must have knocked the gum loose during the night.

My mother returned with what looked like a pair of hedge clippers and went to work. I fidgeted in my chair. It felt like she was doing brain surgery. It must have looked like it, too, because after a minute she stopped and stood there surveying her excavation. "Hmmm. It's worse than I thought. I'll call the beauty shop and see if I can get you an appointment this afternoon."

"Let me stay home today," I pleaded. "I'm already late. Just call school and tell them I'm sick." It wouldn't be far from the truth. My stomach had so many knots in it, it felt like a piece of macramé.

But there was no arguing with my mother. She didn't believe in taking days off unless you had pneumonia, the plague, and chicken pox all together. "I'll drive you on my way to work," she said. "If you brush your hair back into your usual ponytail, it'll be OK for a few hours."

I tried to call Jeanine to tell her what had happened, but nobody answered. I went up to wash what was left of my hair and get ready.

I arrived at my locker about nine-thirty. As soon as I opened the door, it became evident that this was not going to be one of my better days. Everything tumbled out onto the floor. I wanted to cry. I mean, after all, how much could a person take in one morning? A couple of tears started to leak out the corners of my eyes as I sank down in the middle of the mess and began to gather it up.

"Need some help?"

Of course it was Bruce "Two r's" Herrman. I didn't want him to see how close I was to flooding out the entire school, so I just nodded and continued trying to pull my junk — not to mention myself — together.

"I had to fill out some forms in the office," he explained as he retrieved some papers that had sailed to the other side of the hall. I hoped none of my science tests were in there. "I registered this morning, but there were some schedule changes." I let him chat on and watched while he picked up some books and tucked the papers back inside. Like his nose, the rest of him was just about perfect, too. His shoulders were as broad as Jason Kirchfield's, but he had a more casual way of moving. I ducked my head as he came back to the locker.

He bent down, put all the stuff into one pile, then reached out his hand. For a moment, I just stared at it. Then I realized he was offering to help me up. Suddenly my palms got all clammy. Maybe I *was* coming down with pneumonia, etc. But I could hardly ignore him, could I? I let him pull me to my feet. My skin probably felt like raw liver.

"You look kind of different today," he said, not letting go right away. I snatched my hand back. What on earth would Jeanine say if she saw us? It wasn't really fair. I'd been comfortable with the guy the other night at the Castello. Yet here I was, acting dumb just because Angela and Jeanine had turned a simple conversation into the Romance of the Year.

"Uh, thanks," I stammered. I grabbed the books and things away from him and shoved them back into my locker, slamming the door so they wouldn't all come flying out again. "Well, see you later," I said, smiling brightly. Too brightly. I left him standing there with a puzzled look.

I didn't see Jeanine until lunch.

"What happened to you this morning?" she asked

as I sat down at the table. Before I had a chance to answer, she went on. "Guess what? I have Bruce Herrman in all my classes!"

I opened my lunch bag and took out a slightly soggy lettuce and tomato sandwich. "So?"

"I don't know what I'm going to do with you, Mary Frances," she sighed. "Here you have this perfectly nice boy falling all over you and —"

"Let's not start that all over again. He's not falling all over me."

"Well, he said he saw you this morning. That must mean he's interested."

"All it means is that he saw me this morning, Jeanine. You and I are practically the only people he knows in this place."

"I could go for him myself," she went on as if she hadn't heard me, "but Jason walked me into school this morning." Her eyes looked like a planetarium. "I've decided not to give up the fight." She made it sound like we were in the middle of World War III. But a strange feeling had crept up my spine when she'd said that — about going for Bruce herself. I shook it off and tried to distract her by telling her about my problem with the gum.

"Oh, that's awful!" she cried. "Whatever are you going to do?" She was so full of concern, it made me feel like we were back on the same track again. I told her about the appointment at the beauty shop. Right away she wanted to go, too. Maybe I was taking the whole thing about Jason too seriously, I told myself.

My mother picked us up after school. Kicky was in the car, too, because Angela had some kind of meeting and nobody would be home to watch him. I'd almost forgotten that he'd been the cause of all my troubles, but I'd be sure to remember to check my bedposts before I went to sleep from then on.

As soon as we pulled up in front of the Lacy Lady Beauty Salon, Kicky was off and running, dragging my poor mother behind him.

"What's the big hurry?" she asked, finally digging in her heels to slow him down.

"I want to see the cowboys! Maybe they'll have a fight and break chairs over each other's heads like they do on television. Come on!" He tugged impatiently at her hand.

We were all pretty confused by this until I happened to glance up and see the big "Salon" sign hanging over the sidewalk. "That's 'salon,' Kick. Not 'saloon,' " I told him.

"What's the difference?"

I didn't want to go into a vocabulary lesson, so I just said, "It's a French word." He screwed up his face the way he always did when he thought he understood something and then wasn't sure.

"Do they have cowboys in France, too?" he asked.

Even if I had my eyes closed, I could tell I was in a beauty shop the minute the door opened. It smelled damp and sweet, sort of like Angela when she "emerged" from the bathroom. My mother gave me ten dollars and said she was going to do some shopping and would be back in half an hour. She took Kicky with her.

A young girl with apricot-colored hair told me it would be a few minutes and would we please take a seat? In the background, I could see four ladies under the hair dryers. Another one was in a chair with foil spikes sticking out all over her head. "Remember *Battle in Vector Seven?*" I whispered to Jeanine. She glanced over. "The Saturnites." She giggled. I did, too, although I think it was more out of nervousness.

Jeanine picked up a copy of *Stars!* magazine and immediately got lost in a story about Thad Connors, who used to be her big love before Jason Kirchfield came into the picture. I didn't have to read it. It probably told how he lived with his mother in a fourteen-bedroom bungalow in Hollywood, ate raw peanuts and honey for breakfast every day, and was often seen with some up-and-coming young actress. I couldn't help wishing Jeanine still had a crush on him. Being in California, he couldn't complicate my life the way Jason Kirchfield was doing.

"Next?" Apricot Girl was beckoning me. I rose slowly, feeling a little like I was going to the electric chair. But I couldn't walk around with a lump on the back of my head forever, so I sat down in the chair.

Apricot Girl whipped out a long piece of tissue

paper and tied it around my windpipe so tight I could hardly breathe. I stuck my finger up and loosened it while a plastic cape came swooping down over my shoulders.

"We have almost the same color hair," Apricot Girl remarked casually. I wasn't sure about that. Mine was natural. Where hers came from was another matter.

Suddenly the chair spun around and around and I was tipped over backward. I let out a squawk and grabbed the arms to keep from falling. Then my neck hit something hard and hot water rained down on my head, nearly frying my skull. Before I could object, the water went off and Apricot Girl began scrubbing away as if she was trying to get dirt out of an old sock. More hot water, and then I was swung upright, a towel draped over my head. After a few more minutes of having my head nearly shaken off, she began to comb.

"How would you like it done?" she asked. "Oooops! We seem to have a problem back here." Was she kidding? "Well, that makes it easy. Short."

She divided my hair into sections and started snipping away. I could feel the weight dropping off. I couldn't watch. I'd lived with my ponytail too long. I shut my eyes and concentrated instead on the shouting match between the women under the dryers.

". . . and so I said to him, 'If that's the way you feel, you can just pack your bags.' "

"Good for you!"

". . . and then he started crying! Crying, mind you!"

"All done."

This last sentence didn't seem to fit into the conversation, so I looked up into the mirror and immediately clutched my head. What I saw resembled a rock with a giant clump of seaweed attached. My favorite thing.

"It's still wet," Apricot Girl said. "Let me blow it dry a bit."

My ears almost burned off while she brushed and blew and flipped. The next voice I heard was Jeanine's.

"Mary Frances, you're *beautiful!*"

The seaweed-covered rock was gone. In its place was somebody I'd never seen before. If I didn't know it was me sitting there, I'd never have believed it. Soft, coppery ringlets curled all over my head, and little wisps dangled daintily around my ears and down the back of my neck.

"It's a whole new you," cooed Apricot Girl. She gave me a hand mirror and spun me around. The gum and the hole in my head had disappeared. So had the ponytail I'd worn for longer than I remembered. I tipped my head this way and that, still trying to assure myself that it was indeed Mary Frances Courtney looking back at me.

Jeanine could hardly contain herself. My mother,

when she came in a little later, was pleased, too. Kicky, however, echoed my thoughts.

"Mary Frances?" he asked. I had to speak to him before he accepted the fact that I was actually his sister. Then Jeanine had to spoil it.

"Just wait until Bruce Herrman gets a load of this!" she crowed.

Chapter 5

I had to put up with a lot more comments when I got home. Angela oohed and aahed until I was ready to throw up, and even the Apostles had to put their six cents in — two apiece.

"Hey, how about that? She really *is* a girl!"

"What did you think I was — a kangaroo?" I snapped. They made it sound like my parents had suddenly adopted another kid or something. After all, it *was* just a haircut. Although when I thought about it, that probably was a novelty to the Apostles. None of them had seen the inside of a barbershop for months.

Then, during supper, I caught my father watching me once or twice with a funny expression on his face.

Right away I could tell he was thinking he had a second Angela on his hands.

After the table was cleared, I went upstairs and locked myself in the bathroom, which is the only place a person can have any privacy in our house. I guess I wanted to convince myself that I hadn't changed. I looked so different, it was hard to believe I was still the same girl, deep down. Under the vanity light, my curls sent out gleams of a color that somehow seemed closer now to my father's. Even the red splotches weren't quite so noticeable. I touched my hair. It felt all bouncy, and when I pulled at the little wisps, they sproinged right back into place. Jeanine didn't know it, but she'd been right. If Bruce Herrman thought I'd looked different that morning, he sure as heck was going to notice this. Not that I cared, of course, but the thought of it made me smile, for some reason.

Naturally, I hadn't been in there two minutes before Angela was banging at the door.

"Let me in, will you? I have to brush my teeth."

"Hold your horses. Nobody ever got a cavity in three minutes." I flushed the toilet to make it seem like I had a reason for being in there, and unlocked the door.

"Preening?"

"No, I wasn't, Angela. Lay off." I tried to edge past her. She pushed me back into the bathroom.

"Sit down for a minute. I want to talk to you," she

said. It seemed like a funny place to hold a conversation. There wasn't enough room to start getting physical, however. Besides, she was bigger. I sat down on the toilet seat.

Angela perched on the edge of the tub. "Jeanine told me all about this Bruce guy," she began.

"I hope you had a nice chat," I sneered. I started to get up.

"Oh, for Pete's sake, listen to me, will you? It's just that Jeanine's worried that you don't like her anymore. Because she has a boyfriend."

"You'd better check that out with Jason Kirchfield."

"Never mind Jason Kirchfield. The point is, Jeanine is growing up, Mary Frances. It would be nice if you kept her company."

I let out a snort. "And I suppose growing up means you have to go around mooning over boys."

"It's a very natural part of life," said Angela, the Great Expert.

"I don't see Mom and Dad doing it."

She groaned. "Of course they don't. But they did once."

"Angela, Mom and Dad were in their twenties when they got married," I pointed out. "Not thirteen."

"Sure, but how do you suppose Mom knew enough to marry Dad? She just didn't jump at the first guy that came along. You've heard her talk about some of her old boyfriends."

"I've heard Dad talk about them," I said with a snicker. "According to him, they were all short and fat and had buck teeth."

Angela threw up her hands in despair. "Mary Frances, nobody's asking you to date Bruce. You don't even have to like him, although I hear he's pretty cute. Just pretend you do. It would make Jeanine feel like you understand."

Then I exploded. "Well, I *don't* understand! And if you think I'm going to start being dishonest just because of Jeanine, you can go jump in the lake. What she does is her own business. Kindly leave me out of it!"

Her eyes widened. "Why, Mary Frances, I *do* believe you're jealous!"

"*Me?*" I laughed. "What on earth do I have to be jealous about?"

"Because boys are attracted to Jeanine and not you. Only they would be, if you'd just fix yourself up a little."

That did it. I jumped up. The toilet seat came with me, then slammed down again with a bang. I wished Angela's neck was in there. "Listen to me, Angela Courtney," I said as calmly as I could, which wasn't very. "Stop trying to fix me up. I am not a broken-down piece of machinery that everyone has to change little bits and pieces of to make it run better. I operate just fine on my own. And for your information, I have more important things to do than play make-believe with you or Jeanine — or Bruce Herrman either, for that matter."

"Like what?"

Her question stopped me cold. I'd just been mouthing off, the way you do when you get mad. But it suddenly occurred to me as I fumbled for an answer that that was exactly what I was going to have to do — prove that I was grown up. That it could be done without all the silly stages people expect teenagers to go through.

"I don't know!" I shouted finally. "But I'll find something!" With that, I stomped out of the bathroom, slamming the door behind me. Angela could sleep in there, for all I cared.

I raced down the hall, snatching a sweatshirt jacket off one of the bedroom doorknobs. Before I knew it, I was out of the house and running down the sidewalk. The wind cooled my blazing cheeks. I didn't have any idea where I was going. I only wanted to get away — away from Angela, Jeanine, my new haircut, and everything else that was trying to turn me into something I wasn't.

When I stopped to catch my breath, I found myself all the way downtown in the shopping district. There was a small park there. I sank down onto one of the benches, pulled my legs up under me, and buried my face in my knees. Sweat trickled off the ends of my new ringlets and down my forehead. At that point, I wished I could have barged back into the Lacy Lady

Beauty Salon and demanded my ponytail back from Apricot Girl.

The inside of my head felt like a clothes dryer, with a bundle of thoughts tumbling around and around inside. And every once in a while, like a red shirt flashing by the dryer window, floated the perfectly straight nose of Bruce "Two *r*'s" Herrman. I squeezed my eyes shut to blot it out. It didn't belong there.

I sat for hours, it seemed, but no ideas came. How was I supposed to convince people they were wrong about me? Again, that crazy longing swept over me to go back to the days when Jeanine and I held tea parties for our dolls in the backyard. Life had been so much easier then. But that, I had to keep reminding myself, was impossible.

At last I gave up trying to sort it all out. It was beginning to get dark, and the sweat inside my jacket was making me chilly. I stood up, jammed my hands in my pockets, and started home. For the first time, I noticed that the sweatshirt I was wearing must have belonged to one of the Apostles. It hung down almost to my knees. I must have looked like a scarecrow flopping along down the street.

Inside the pocket, my fingers closed around a piece of paper. Well, even with all my problems, I guess I'm as curious as the next person. I pulled it out, unfolded it and read.

It was not, as I guess I sort of hoped, a love note. It was a printed form. CHILDREN'S HOSPITAL 20

MILE MARATHON. Under the caption, it told how each runner was to get sponsors to pledge a certain amount for each mile he ran. The paper was obviously Matt's. He'd been busy, too. The page was almost completely filled. I may not have been too hot in science, but my math was good enough. Even without a pencil, I figured that if Matt finished the twenty miles, he'd earn about three hundred dollars. Depending on how many runners were entered, the hospital could end up making an awful lot of money.

I put the paper back in the pocket. It depressed me even more. Here he was, my own brother, doing something worthwhile. Why couldn't I? Maybe they'd let me enter the race, but as soon as the thought came, I realized I could never run twenty miles.

I sighed and continued on my way, dragging my feet along the pavement. When I reached the corner, I checked for traffic. Suddenly, my eyes lit on a building across the street. It was the library. Seeing it made me think again about Kicky and how he was going to miss his Walt Disney movies. Then something started chewing at the edges of my mind. I stood there, balanced on the curb, until it took shape.

Of course! The library needed money. Certainly not as much, I was pretty sure. Why couldn't there be a runathon for that? But could I do it? I didn't know anything about organizing such a big project, but I sure did know where I could go for help! Wouldn't that be a great way to prove my point?

I threw my arms around him and gave him a big hug.

"Hey, don't muss up my locks!" he yelled. "I just got them the way I want them."

I giggled. "You're beginning to sound like Angela."

"Horrors! A worse fate there never was!"

I left him and went straight to my desk. From the drawer I took out an old notebook, ripped out the used pages and jotted down all the things Matt had told me. Tomorrow, right after school, I'd go and see Mr. Muldoon. Maybe he'd help me organize it. If he liked the idea, that is.

I was deep in thought when Angela came in.

"Get over your snit?"

I grinned to myself, closed the cover of my notebook and stood up. "Snit?" I gave her my most dazzling smile. "Whatever made you think I was in a snit?"

She looked suspicious. "You mean you're not mad?"

"Certainly not! As a matter of fact, Angela, you have just done me the biggest favor of my life. Let's have these little chats more often, OK?"

You could tell she was confused. For the first time since I could remember, she went to bed without biting off her nail polish.

Chapter 6

"Come in, please." With a slight bow, Mr. Muldoon ushered me into his office.

The room was small and neat, except for the top of his desk. Files of papers and books covered the top, and sticking up out of the mess was a framed picture of a pretty woman holding a little boy in a sailor suit. There wasn't much doubt about who the kid was. Put a pair of dark-rimmed glasses on him and he'd be Mr. Muldoon's twin. He did have a bit more hair, though.

I sank down into the chair Mr. Muldoon had pulled out for me. I was exhausted. School that day had been pretty traumatic, what with not being able to take three steps without somebody or other commenting on my haircut. Even most of the teachers noticed it.

At lunch, Jeanine had presided over the table as if she'd been the one who'd created the miracle. "Isn't it just *darling?*" she kept saying until I wanted to kick her. "I've been telling her how great she'd look with it short, but she never believed me." Personally, I only remembered her saying anything of the sort once, and that was the day my ponytail got caught in my gymsuit zipper.

Of Bruce "Two *r*'s" Herrman, there'd been no sign, much to my relief. Once or twice I thought I saw him in the hall, but I never got close enough to find out. It was strange, though. Each time, I got the funniest feeling — almost like disappointment. Only I knew it couldn't be that.

The only thing that made the whole day the least bit bearable was getting a $B+$ on my science paper. Up at the top, Mrs. Novelli had scribbled: "Good job — and a nice change from the Curies." My father would be happy.

Mr. Muldoon perched on the edge of his desk, looking even more like an owl than ever, what with the papers and things making sort of a nest. "Now, how may I be of assistance, Miss — uh — Courtney?" he asked.

I squirmed in my chair. I'd thought out the whole idea of the marathon pretty carefully during study period. The only thing I hadn't done was figured out what to say. Suddenly, sitting there face-to-face with

Mr. Muldoon, my great plan seemed dumb. The man obviously didn't even remember me.

"Uh," I stammered, which wasn't exactly the most brilliant thing I could have come up with, "uh, I was talking to you last Saturday about the Walt Disney movies being canceled."

"Yes?" He glanced at the watch, then at me.

"Uh," I said again. I took a deep breath, then plunged on. "Well, you said the library didn't have enough money for the program."

"That's correct."

He wasn't making this any easier. "I — uh — I had this idea that might help you raise enough to continue the movies."

Above his glasses, his eyebrows drew together like two caterpillars inching along the grass.

"My brother Matt is running in the City Children's Hospital Marathon this weekend," I went on quickly. "He was telling me about it and I was wondering if the library couldn't do the same thing." I yanked my notebook from my stack of books and flipped it open to the pages I'd worked over during school. "I made a list of what would have to be done." I handed Mr. Muldoon the notebook. "I mean, I was just wondering . . ." I trailed off, not knowing what else to add.

He took it and began reading. I fidgeted in my seat. I still thought it would work, but that was only natural, I guess, since I'd been the one to come up with it. It might not look so terrific to James Muldoon, Library Director.

It didn't take him long to finish. After he was done, he dropped the notebook on his desk, took off his glasses and started polishing them on his sleeve. Then he shook his head.

My heart sank. He didn't like it! How could I have been so idiotic as to think I could solve all the library's financial problems in one night? Who did I think I was, anyway?

Mr. Muldoon replaced his glasses. "Why people cast such disparaging remarks about our younger generation, I'll never comprehend," he said, still shaking his head. "This alone would disprove them."

All the breath I didn't realize I was holding came out in one gasp. It almost sounded as if —

"What a simply delicious idea!" Mr. Muldoon chortled, if I have my word right. "Young lady, I congratulate you on your intelligence."

Suddenly I found myself smiling all over the place. There hadn't been anything too humorous about my life during the past few days, and it sure felt good. I wished I could take him to Mrs. Novelli's class for Show and Tell.

Mr. Muldoon rose and went around the desk to sit in his chair. "Pull your seat up here, Miss Courtney, and let's hear what you have in mind."

I spilled it all out, everything that had been churning around in my head half the night and most of the day. "Well," I began, "I thought that since this money will be mostly used for kids, they could be the ones who would earn it. It wouldn't be twenty miles like the hospital marathon, naturally, but maybe five. And," I added, really getting warmed up, "if the little ones couldn't run, they could walk only a mile or two."

Mr. Muldoon mulled that over. "Hmmmm. I think I understand. Sort of a 'Children for Children.' Is that the general drift?"

He spoke in kind of an old-fashioned way, but I liked it. Not that I always understood all the words he used, but the meaning came through all right. Obviously he had trouble putting his thoughts into words of less than four syllables.

"Kids for Kids," I suggested.

He laughed. "Yes. That has a little more . . ."

"Pizzazz," I supplied.

"Exactly."

There were only a couple of hitches. "Because of certain unforeseen financial problems," he told me, "not only have we had to cancel the movie program, but we also have a reduced staff. I couldn't release anyone to devote time to a project of this magnitude. In fact, I'm afraid the only way we could manage it is if you were willing to handle the majority of the work. Maybe some of your friends could help. We'd do everything in our power to assist you, of course. What do you say?"

"But I want to do it myself!" I exclaimed. It was going to be a big job. Bigger than I'd ever imagined. But wasn't that the whole reason behind it? I thought. I had a point to prove. No fairy godmother was going to pop up out of the pumpkin patch and do it for me, that was for sure.

"Excellent," Mr. Muldoon declared.

The other problem had to do with getting the library's Board of Trustees to approve the project.

"They're the ones with the decision-making authority, you see," he explained. "I shouldn't think that will be too difficult a hurdle, however. I've never known them to look a gift horse in the mouth, so to speak."

The board would be meeting later in the week, he said, and he'd bring it up then.

"But I don't see any reason why we shouldn't proceed on the assumption it will be approved."

We worked for about half an hour. By the time we were finished, it was nearly five o'clock, but we'd covered just about every angle either of us could think of, including setting a tentative date.

"School will be out on June twenty-fourth," I suggested. "We could hold it that Saturday. Then exams would be over, and most families don't usually go on vacation until July."

He agreed.

I was to be in charge of making posters, of coordinating with the schools and getting permission from the town council and the police department. Mr. Muldoon offered the use of the library's duplicating machines to print the forms. We would meet in a week or two to check on my progress.

My head was spinning when I left the library. It suddenly occurred to me that it had been nearly an hour and a half since I'd worried about my hair, Jeanine, Bruce Herrman, and all the other stuff that had been bothering me lately. This runathon was going to be just what the doctor ordered. From now on, I'd be so busy I wouldn't have time to think about anything else.

Earlier in the day, Jeanine had asked me if I'd help her with some math homework that night, so after supper I walked over to her house. Jeanine's parents had been divorced a few years ago. She and her mother lived in a totally spotless house that always made me a bit uncomfortable. I mean, it had white shag rugs all over the downstairs — except the kitchen, naturally. I always took off my shoes at the door, even though nobody ever told me to. I couldn't imagine ever having a place like that. My family needed wall-to-wall concrete.

Jeanine's mom, who was a secretary for some law firm, had to work late that night, so the two of us were alone. After we finished the math — it took Jeanine an hour to understand that when you multiplied a negative number by another negative, you got a positive — Jeanine made a batch of popcorn and opened a couple of bottles of cola.

"Now I only have one more subject to worry about," she said as we munched our way through the bowl.

"As long as it isn't science," I said.

"Not that kind of subject, silly. I just have to figure out what to wear to the dance on Friday."

I should have known. "Jeanine, I've seen your closet. You have more clothes than a department store."

"I know, but Jason's seen everything I own."

"So what?"

"This is very special, Mary Frances. It's my first real date."

Half a date, I thought to myself, remembering Jason's promise to Sarah Proefrock.

"What are you wearing?" Jeanine continued.

"Me? Who said I was even going?"

She stared at me as if I'd just turned into the Loch Ness Monster. Then she gave a nervous laugh. "You're kidding, right?"

"Wrong. This is your date, not mine. What am I supposed to do while you're waltzing around with Jason? Stand on my head in the corner?"

"But I can't go by myself!" she cried. She sounded sort of panicky.

She was right, I guess. I tried to put myself in her

shoes. It was hard because I knew I'd never be wasting my time over something so unimportant as a boy. But then, I reminded myself, to Jeanine, Jason *was* important. It wouldn't be fair of me to dump her, just because I didn't happen to see things the same way. If I was really her friend, I'd stick by her, no matter what. "I *am* just teasing, Jeanine," I said finally. "I'm going."

"Oh, I knew you were," she said, relief breaking out all over her. She leaned over the table. "My mom said I could wear some makeup. Just a little, of course. My eyes, that's all. Want to try some? I have it up in my room."

"No, thanks," I said hastily. Enough was enough.

She persisted. "It would look really great, Mary Frances. You'd sweep Bruce Herrman right off his feet."

"Jeanine —"

"OK. I'll stop. But he's one cute guy, Mary Frances, and you have a head start on anybody else. You ought to think about it."

Although I sure wasn't going to mention it to Jeanine, that was one of my problems. I *was* thinking about that perfectly straight nose, more than I cared to admit, even to myself. Once my runathon got off the ground, it would disappear. I was convinced of that.

But on the way home, I couldn't help wondering if Bruce was going to be there on Friday. What would it be like to actually dance with him? I guess I was dreaming a bit because I walked right into a tree and then said, "Excuse me," to it.

In a way, I was worse than the cat in the cartoon. The snowball had hit me — SMACK — and was carrying me along with it. The trouble was, I didn't even know it.

Chapter 7

I must have been crazy to think that just because things had settled down somewhat, they were going to stay that way forever. Jeanine was crying again, and doing her best to soak every available inch of paper towel in the North Valley Junior High girls' john. Through the wall, the throbbing beat of a bass guitar was giving me an even bigger headache than the one I already had.

"Jeanine, calm down," I pleaded, tossing the fifth chunk of soggy brown paper toward the trash. "You're getting your blouse all wet."

"Is that all you can think of?" she moaned. "My whole life is in ruins and you're worried about a dumb old rag?" The "dumb old rag" was brand new and had cost thirty dollars.

The reason for Jeanine's hysterics was — who else? — Jason Kirchfield. The dance had begun over an hour ago and no Jason had appeared to float away with Jeanine in his arms. (Every other dance, of course.) At first, she hadn't thought much about it, figuring he was just late. She'd chatted with the other girls and even danced a little, but as time went on, I could see her getting more and more nervous. Her eyes kept flitting back and forth to the door and she even turned down an invitation from some guy that, somebody whispered, was a *tenth grader*. The final blow had come when Laura Hubert casually mentioned that she'd seen Jason talking with Sarah Proefrock in front of Barcelona's Deli after school. Since Sarah was also among the missing, Jeanine was now convinced the two of them had eloped, or something equally drastic. That would have suited me just fine, but I was never that lucky.

A couple of girls wandered into the john just then. They eyed Jeanine's obvious state of agitation, nodded knowingly at each other, and disappeared into the stalls. If I was Jeanine, I'd have been embarrassed, but she didn't seem to notice.

I waited until the place cleared out again and continued my efforts to calm her down. "This isn't exactly what I'd planned for the evening," I remarked sarcastically. "We've been in here ten minutes, Jeanine. Why don't we just go home?"

Her head whipped up, spraying tears in every direction. "Go home? What if Jason comes?"

"I thought he eloped."

"Don't be stupid, Mary Frances." She sniffed. "He's much too young."

That's what I liked about Jeanine. She's so consistent. "Well, then, let's go out and see if the king has honored us with his presence."

Her eyes narrowed. "One would think you didn't even like Jason."

"Heaven forbid. I *adore* him. Doesn't everybody?"

Fortunately, she didn't take that the way I meant it. "I guess you're right," she said at last. "There's probably a very good reason why he's late." She mopped up the rest of the tears, then surveyed herself in the mirror. "I'm a *mess!*" She turned on the tap and started splashing water on her face. At the rate she was going, her skin was going to shrivel up like a prune.

Knowing Jeanine, it would take her another half hour to make herself presentable. I was tired, among other things, of standing, and my headache wasn't helping. I told her I'd wait outside.

The stairs leading to the second floor classrooms were opposite the john, so I sat down on the bottom step and rested my head against the cool tiled walls. Through the gym doors, the dance was still going strong. A bunch of couples were jumping up and down in the middle of the floor. Along the sides, like spectators at a basketball game, was another mob. Everyone seemed to be having a good time, which was more than I was doing, I thought, closing my eyes.

After my talk with Mr. Muldoon, life had gone back to normal. People gradually became accustomed to my new hairstyle, as I had, and even Jeanine had stopped her campaign to pair me off with Bruce "Two r's" Herrman. Since Angela was busy with her plans for the Junior Prom, she was off my back for the moment, too.

Mr. Muldoon had called on Thursday with the news that the Board of Trustees had been "very receptive" to my idea for the runathon. They'd even approved a small budget so I could buy what I needed for the posters. Mr. Muldoon also told me he planned to contact the *North Valley Sentinel,* our town newspaper, to see if they'd be interested in doing a story on me and the runathon. I balked a bit when he said that. The last thing I wanted was for people to think I was doing it for the publicity. But after he pointed out that it would help the project, I reluctantly agreed to be interviewed.

I'd already mapped out some of my strategy for getting people signed up. Each school building would have a signup sheet in the office. After all, it was for education in a way, wasn't it? And John was good at drawing, so I planned to ask him for some help with the posters. I still hadn't told anyone what I was doing. Not even Jeanine. I doubted if she could get her mind off Jason Kirchfield long enough to listen. And, too, until everything was in place, there wasn't much sense in making a big deal out of it.

"Wear yourself out already?"

I sat up so fast that I banged my head on the metal railing of the stairs. Little lights went dancing across my eyes. When I could focus again, there sat Bruce "Two r's" Herrman, accompanied by his absolutely gorgeous nose, on the step beside me.

"Sorry," he said. "I didn't mean to scare you. Are you all right?" He reached out his hand and touched my head. I jumped as if a thousand volts of electricity had gone through me.

"Don't!" I yelped. I knew it wasn't just my head. It hurt, but not that much. "I mean, I'm all right. Really."

He leaned back against the upper stair and casually stuck his hands in his pockets. "I just got here," he said. "I was supposed to come with Jason, but then he got sick."

"Jason's sick?" Jeanine was going to be interested in that piece of news.

"The flu or something, I guess. Anyway, I thought I'd stay home, since I didn't know anybody, and then I decided it beat watching cops-and-robbers shows on TV."

If my brain had been working normally, I might

have said something like "I'm glad you did" or "Yes, it's a good chance to meet some kids." But my tongue couldn't locate anything that made sense, and I just sat there like a stuffed animal.

"I haven't seen you around school the last couple of days," he said.

I could feel the red splotches rising. Had he been looking for me? I was as bad as Jeanine. "I've been busy," I said abruptly.

"Oh." He let it go at that. I glanced at the john door. Wasn't Jeanine ever going to come out? I mean, what was I supposed to do? Bruce didn't offer any more comments either, and it kept getting quieter and quieter. Even the noise pouring out of the gym faded into the background.

Then Bruce said, "You know, I like your hair that way."

I froze. What on earth could I answer to that? I was beginning to get even more flustered when he added, "Jeanine told me what happened. With the gum, I mean. My little sister did the same thing once."

His little sister! Boy, did that make me feel like the klutz of the week! Trust Jeanine to go spreading that story around school. How many other people were having a good laugh at my expense? Not that this wasn't enough!

I jumped up, unable to take the strain any longer. "Well, I have to go," I said brightly and hurried across the hall to the john. I was halfway there when it hit me what I'd said. I mean, considering where I was headed and all. You just don't go around discussing your personal habits in front of boys. I threw open the door, nearly smashing Jeanine into the wall.

"What's the matter?" she cried, following me back to the sink.

"Nothing." I grabbed for a paper towel. Naturally, there weren't any left. "I just bumped my head."

"Let me see. There isn't a lump or anything." Then she caught sight of my face and burst out laughing. "We make a great pair. You look like you're ready to cry, too."

"Well, I'm not," I said furiously. "Let's go home, Jeanine. Jason isn't going to be here. He has the flu."

"Who told you that?"

"Bruce Herrman."

That did it. "You saw Bruce?" she squeaked as if he was a UFO. "Where?"

"Out there. In the hall."

"Did he ask you to dance?"

"The dance is in the gym, Jeanine."

"But . . ."

"Come on. Let's go." I pulled at her. "Hurry."

"No." She took a deep breath and announced, "I've just decided that I'm not going to let Jason get me down anymore. Like Angela said, there are a lot of other fish in the sea."

It sure was a great time for her to get interested in marine life. I didn't care to spend the whole rest of the night avoiding Bruce Herrman. I tried to talk her out of staying, but she wouldn't listen to reason. She was going to go out there and have a great time, Jason or no Jason.

She meant what she said, too. We hadn't been back in the gym two minutes before she was dancing away. I guess I should have been thankful she'd finally come to her senses about Jason, but I'd learned that she had more ups and downs than a toad. Tomorrow there would probably be another crisis.

I stood around talking with Patti Hodgeson and some of her friends for a while. I didn't have much to say because all they wanted to discuss was who was going out with who and what guys were worth looking at. I pretended to be interested, though, and waited for the night to end.

Suddenly, through the crowd, I saw Jeanine dancing with Bruce Herrman. It was a slow number and she was nestled in his arms. Bruce's chin rested lightly on top of her golden head. They reminded me of a fairy-tale prince and princess.

A surge of bitterness swept through me. What was the matter with Jeanine? Hadn't she ever heard of loyalty? It obviously didn't bother her that poor Jason might possibly be at death's door, or, for that matter, that I was standing there twiddling my thumbs. She was off in her own little world.

"Mary Frances, you look like you're about to punch someone." Patti was laughing and pointing to my hands, which I suddenly noticed were clenched into fists, the knuckles showing white through my skin. Then she, too, caught sight of Jeanine and Bruce. "Ah, I see. The little green devil."

That was absolutely the most ridiculous thing I'd ever heard. Little green devils meant jealousy, and I certainly wasn't guilty of that.

Or was I?

The thought astounded me so much that I actually lost my balance and stepped backward onto somebody's foot.

"Sorry," I murmured.

Angela had mentioned jealousy, too, but I'd just put it down as a figment of her imagination, which was always working overtime anyway. I'd never let anything come between Jeanine and me. Not after we'd spent practically our entire lives together. And especially not over something as unimportant as a boy. Yet, as I stood there watching her and Bruce, I couldn't deny it any longer. I didn't want it to be Jeanine out there in Bruce's arms. I wanted it to be me!

When the music stopped, Jeanine grabbed Bruce's hand and pulled him over to where we were.

"Look who I found!" she chirped.

Naturally, everyone swarmed around him and wanted to know how he liked North Valley and where he came from and so on. I was still so shaken by my feelings that I turned aside, wishing I was anyplace else but there. Even home, watching a Jacques Cousteau special on seaweed.

"Want to dance?"

The voice in my ear could only belong to one person. Bruce Herrman. With a start I realized that the music had begun again. Another slow number.

I was glad I had my back to him so he couldn't see my face, which was splotching all over, I was sure. Isn't this exactly what you wanted? I asked myself fiercely. Now it's *your* turn to be the princess!

On legs that had suddenly turned into pieces of cooked macaroni, I turned — only to see Bruce "Two r's" Herrman and his gorgeous nose leading Patti Hodgeson onto the dance floor.

Chapter 8

Except for the steady rhythm of chicken bones hitting Mark's plate, the dining room was as quiet as a classroom when the principal drops in unexpectedly. All eyes were focused on Angela, standing in the doorway. In her hands was the *North Valley Sentinel* and she was staring at it as if it was a live boa constrictor.

My mother broke the silence. "Mark, stop eating like a barbarian. Your plate looks like a cemetery."

"Tell us what's so breathtaking in the headlines, Angela," my father said. "Has there been another political scandal? Or, worse yet, is there a big sale on at Berkeley's Department Store?"

The Apostles let out a collective snort.

"Can I buy a pair of scandals?" asked Kicky. "It's almost summer."

I giggled.

At that moment, the phone rang. My father sighed. "Can't we have one meal without that thing going off?"

Angela never moved.

"I'll get it," I said.

"Oh, Mary Frances, what are you going to do?" Jeanine's voice, on the edge of hysteria, came over the receiver.

"Do? About what?" I asked.

"You mean you haven't seen it?"

"Seen what?"

"The paper! Your picture is on the front page, and —"

"It is?" The front page! Wow! Mr. Muldoon hadn't been kidding when he said he was going to get some publicity. A reporter had called a few days before and I'd given him all the information, but I never dreamed he was going to make such a big deal out of it. This was even better than I'd hoped. I grinned to myself. "Well, what do you think of it?" I asked Jeanine, anxious to get her reaction.

"It's a great idea, Mary Frances. Really. But —"

"Never mind. Don't tell me. I want to read it myself. I'll call you back later, OK?"

"But, Mary Frances —"

"What?"

"Uh — nothing. Just make sure you're sitting down when you read it."

I hung up, wondering what in the world she meant. Maybe the picture was lousy. Newspapers have a way of making people look like they're a hundred years old. It didn't matter, though. Now my project was official. I guess it was crazy of me, but I still hadn't mentioned it to anyone. I'd wanted to make sure it was really going to happen.

On Monday, after school, I'd been out in front trimming the gardens when a car pulled up and this guy with a camera climbed out.

"Courtney house?" he asked. When I nodded, he said, "There's some kid I'm supposed to get a picture of. Something about the library. I should have called, but since I was passing by on my way to another assignment, I thought I'd stop and see if I could save myself a trip."

It was news to me. The reporter hadn't mentioned anything about a picture. It wasn't really necessary. But, I'd reminded myself, it wouldn't hurt to attract a little more attention. Parents read the paper. Maybe they'd talk their kids into entering the runathon. So I'd agreed.

I was in my old GO FLY A KITE sweatshirt. I suggested changing, but then the photographer said they'd just be using a head shot anyway and it wouldn't make any difference. I ran my fingers through my hair a couple of times and said, "Cheese."

No wonder Angela had acted so surprised. It wasn't every day she saw her sister's picture in the paper. She probably never thought I was capable of doing something so spectacular. It might take her a month to recover from the shock.

Nobody looked at me when I went back into the dining room, except Kicky, who greeted me with "Do I have to call you Frankie now?"

"Hush up!" Angela hissed, digging him in the ribs with her elbow.

"Ow! That hurt, Angela!" Kicky punched her back. "Do I, Mary Frances?"

"I don't know what you're talking about," I replied. "Can I see the paper, Angela? Where is it?"

"You'd better eat your dinner first," she mumbled. "You're going to need your strength."

Something was definitely wrong. I glanced at my mother. She looked a little sad. "What's going on?" I demanded. "And where's the paper?"

Without a word, Matt handed the folded front section across the table. I scanned it, bubbling out loud, "Did you all see it? Just imagine! The front page! I didn't —" And then I spotted it. "Oh, my God! What did they *do*?" I cried.

It wasn't the picture. That hadn't turned out too bad, aside from the fact that my hair looked gray. The terrible thing was a few spaces down.

Frankie Runs for Library

The headline was big and black as if they were announcing the cure for the common cold. "Now how on earth did they come up with that name?" I yelled.

"Read it," muttered Angela. "It gets worse."

So I did. And it did.

> *A North Valley teenager has come up with an idea to help fund the public library's children's film program, abandoned recently because of financial difficulties.*
>
> *James Muldoon, Library Director, told* The Sentinel *that Francis Courtney, 13, an eighth grade student at North Valley Junior High, approached him last week about the possibility of sponsoring a runathon, the proceeds of which will go to support the Saturday afternoon film presentations. Already, Muldoon said, the library's Board of Trustees has approved the project.*
>
> *Young Courtney said he had been inspired by last week's successful fund-raiser for the City Children's Hospital after his six-year-old brother missed the weekly Walt Disney movies. He said . . .*

I couldn't go on. It was too awful. How could they have ever mistaken me for a *boy?*

Matt cleared his throat, carefully wiped the barbecue sauce off his moustache, and said, "If it makes any difference, we all think you're pretty special."

"Amen," echoed my father fervently.

I knew what they were trying to say and I appreciated it. I really did. But somehow all the problems I'd been running into during the past couple of weeks came boiling up inside me again and the pressure was just too much.

"I wish I'd never even *thought* of it!" I cried, and ran from the room.

Upstairs, I buried my face in my pillow and let the tears flow. Wasn't my life ever going to straighten itself out? First it had been all that nonsense with Jeanine over Jason Kirchfield, then the disaster when Kicky left the gum on my bedpost. To top it off, I couldn't seem to cope with my strange new feelings, especially about Bruce Herrman. I hadn't needed that complication. But it was happening, despite what I wanted.

For days after the dance, I'd walked around feeling like somebody had stepped on my stomach. Instead of becoming the princess in Bruce's arms, I'd ended up the court jester.

Only by throwing all my energy into planning the runathon was I able to snap out of it a bit. Now *this*.

How was I ever going to hold up my head in public again? I think if that reporter had been around just then, I'd have kicked his typewriter into a million pieces and tied him up with the ribbon. As a matter of fact, if I remember right, I did take my pillow and practice up. It made me feel a little better, but not much.

Angela stuck her head around the corner of the doorway. "Can I come in?" she asked cautiously.

I wiped my face on the spread and sat up. "It's your room."

"Oh, yeah. I guess it is." She gave a nervous laugh and stepped in. "How are you feeling?"

"About how you'd expect if you'd been called a boy in the local newspaper." She shuddered. I could tell the very thought of it gave her the creeps. Not that she had to worry.

She fussed around with the bottles on her nightstand for a minute or two, as if she was trying to get up the courage to say something, and then finally she did. "I know this might not be the right time, Mary Frances, but you really did bring it on yourself."

Trust Angela. I wondered if she poisoned dogs in her spare time. "And just how did you come to that conclusion?" I asked.

"Well, you run around in those scruffy jeans and those ugly sweatshirts all the time, expecting people to just assume you're a girl. There isn't anything feminine about you."

I stared at her for a long moment. For once, Angela had gone one step too far with her big sister act. I tried, but I couldn't control myself. "Thank you, Miss America," I said through clenched teeth. "I really appreciate your kind words. Now, would you like to hear what I think about you? I'll tell you anyway. I think you're the most selfish individual on the face of this planet. You think the world ought to be full of little Angela robots, who walk and talk and look just like you. It never occurred to that pea brain of yours that some people want to be different."

"But I didn't think —"

"You never do. You just let your mouth flap around like a dust rag. Right now I'm miserable enough without you making it worse. Why don't you do some growing up yourself? You might find life interesting as a human being!"

I stormed out, slamming the door behind me. Maybe my anger would jar some sense into her, although I doubted it. People like Angela never want to believe they're wrong about anything.

I went down to the kitchen to try and calm down with a glass of cold milk. My father was at the table reading the paper. He waited until I'd drained the glass, then spoke.

"Want to talk about it?"

I wiped my mouth with my sleeve. "What's there to talk about? I'm dead."

"Pretty lively corpse."

"I'll have to move to Timbuktu," I muttered darkly.

"Have you thought about changing jobs lately?"

He laughed. I guess I did, too. "Occasionally. But not for that reason. I'm afraid you're just going to have to stick it out."

"How can I?" I cried, my momentary good humor gone. "I'll be the laughingstock of the whole town."

"Come on. It isn't all that bad."

"Oh, no?"

"Anyway, is it that important?"

How could he ask that? Maybe he didn't remember what it was like to be young. "Of course it's important," I said.

"More important than the fact that you stand to make a lot of people happy? And not only Kicky, either."

"But —"

"But what?"

"I'm afraid nobody will take me seriously now. The runathon is going to turn into one big joke."

"Actions speak louder than words."

"Not those ones. The ones in the paper, I mean." Just thinking about it made me grit my teeth.

"Mary Frances —"

"Don't you mean 'Frankie'?" I couldn't help it. It just came out.

"NO!" He shouted it, and then his face began to get red splotches, just like mine. Funny, I never noticed he had that problem, too. "Honey," he said more calmly, "you're still my girl. That's G.I.R.L. Nothing's going to change that. It's pure biological fact, and time will show you how true it is."

"That's easy for you to say. You never —"

"Oh, didn't I?" He tilted back on his chair. "Let me tell you a little story. When I was about your age, I had this awful high-pitched voice. People used to think I was my mother when I answered the phone."

"They did?" It was hard to believe, listening now to his deep baritone. "What did you do about it?"

He chuckled. "For a while, I got into a great many unnecessary fights. When I was fifteen, it got even worse. I couldn't say two words without my voice changing in midstream. But eventually I made it through. Just like you're going to do. You can't un-print the newspaper, but you can turn it to your advantage."

"How?"

"Let them have their fun. They're going to, anyway. Go along with it. Then, when they're finished, put them on the spot and sign them up. That article has probably saved you a lot of work."

"Have you ever been in a junior high lately?"

"Not if I could help it. But old and decrepit though I may be, I think I know human nature. Kids haven't changed that much. Oh, the clothes are different and the music is a bit louder — a lot louder — but underneath, I think you'll find they really want to help."

I thought about what he'd said for the rest of the night. One thing was for sure. I'd started something, and I couldn't very well go crying back to Mr. Muldoon and say I'd changed my mind. I was going to have to finish it, no matter how rough it got.

And boy, was it getting rough!

Chapter 9

"Hey, Frankie!"

I looked around. By this time it was getting as automatic as breathing. Jason Kirchfield, miraculously with no girl hanging on his arm, was headed down the hall in my direction, giving me a splendid view of his inflated chest. I wished I had a pin.

"Hi, Jason," I said.

"Hi." With Jason, I figured that might be the end of the conversation, but he surprised me. "Hey, are you still doing that — uh —" he struggled "— run-athon thing?"

"Sure." I flashed him a smile. It almost hurt, but sometimes you have to make sacrifices, I told myself. "Why?"

"Well, — uh, I don't know if you know it, but I'm into sports pretty heavy."

I couldn't resist it. "You *are?*"

"Uh, yeah. I'm in pretty good shape." Oh, lord, was he going to flex his muscles at me? My opinion of Jeanine's intelligence sank even lower.

He hesitated, as if waiting for me to drop before his feet in a dead faint. When I didn't, he seemed confused. "Can I sign up?"

As irritating as Jason was, one thing was for sure. I was willing to bet he could run five miles. Every dollar counted. "Why, Jason," I cooed, "that's *wonderful.*" I fished around in my jeans pocket, came up with the signup sheet that was becoming as much a part of me as my freckles and pointed to a blank line. "Just put your John Hancock right there."

He blinked.

"Write your name," I sighed.

He scribbled something unreadable and handed it back. "Hey, I'm playing ball tomorrow at Wakelyn Park. Wanna come watch me?"

About as much as I wanted an appendix operation. "Sorry, Jason, but I'm not — uh, into sports," I said. "I'll get your sponsor sheets to you after school. They're in my locker."

He was looking vague again. Jeanine might be able to get some mileage of her own out of this. He'd probably need a tutor to help him figure out what he was supposed to do.

On my way to English class, I glanced again at the sheet. It was getting filled up, and it was my third one. My father's predictions had come true. At first, it had been hard — the day after the article appeared in the *Sentinel*, especially. My face was almost permanently red from all the teasing. Most of the girls, though, had been sympathetic.

"You're so brave, Mary Frances," Patti Hodgeson had remarked. "I'd never set foot in school again if that happened to me." Plus, of course, she'd signed up for the runathon. So did a lot of others.

Altogether, my lists now had a total of twenty-four names. No, twenty-five, counting Jason. And that didn't include the sheets I'd left in the senior high and elementary school offices. If I could count on every person getting at least five sponsors, and if each sponsor pledged at least fifty cents a mile, I already had a good start on the thousand dollars Mr. Muldoon had estimated it would cost for the film program. And I still had two weeks to go.

Other good things had happened, too. The reporter from the *Sentinel* had called the next afternoon to apologize for the article. He felt pretty bad. He said he'd been out that day and because the paper needed the write-up, another reporter had used his notes.

"I scribble," he confessed. "He must have read it wrong."

No kidding.

Since it hadn't really hurt anything but my feelings,

I told him to forget it. He insisted on printing a retraction, though. And to make up for the mix-up, he also promised to help get some television coverage for the runathon. Maybe it had all been worthwhile, after all.

The entire next weekend had been spent on making posters. John, bless his little heart, helped. They turned out really cute. He drew these neat little books with feet on them, running across a finish line, arms up in the air like when you win a race. The books even had sneakers on. The Apostles took turns driving me around to different stores, so I could put the posters up. The store owners were all cooperative and wished me luck. I even signed a few of them up to be my sponsors.

The most surprising result of my efforts, though — one which I hadn't counted on, but which made me very, very happy — was that Jeanine became almost as enthusiastic as I was. Not only had she stood by me during all the teasing, but she also pitched in in other places.

"You're so disorganized," she said to me one day when I was wrestling with a bunch of paperwork. "You need a secretary."

"Right. And just where do you suggest I find one?" I grumbled.

"Me."

"You?" Then suddenly I remembered that Jeanine's mother had taught her to type when she was nine years old. Jeanine always had the neatest papers of anybody in school. I threw the mess at her. "You are looking at one person who would be eternally grateful. If," I added sourly, "it isn't a hopeless case."

"Nothing is that hopeless," she said, and in short order she had everything put together so that a kindergartner could find his way through it. She also typed the letters to the school board, and to the town council asking their permission to use the streets. Which, of course, they granted. And to the police, who agreed to put up barricades and generally keep their eyes on things. It felt like old times, the two of us working together.

Strangely enough, during all that time, Jeanine hardly ever mentioned Jason Kirchfield. Since she hadn't mentioned anyone else, either, I figured she was still madly in love with Jason, but at least I didn't have to listen to daily reports of the ups and downs of their relationship, such as it was.

As for myself, I was too busy to worry about anything, including Bruce "Two r's" Herrman. Besides all the extra work of organizing the runathon, there were final exams to study for. Every night, I prayed to Florence Rena Sabin to help me pass science. Surely she'd understand how hard it was, even if Mrs. Novelli didn't.

Then, too, there was the running. I didn't want to embarrass myself in front of half the town by crawling part of the way on my hands and knees during the runathon. Most of the time Matt went with me, and sometimes even Jeanine joined us on our jaunts around the block. She'd usually do one lap, though, then sit on our front step and rest until we came around again. If we'd been jogging on Jason Kirchfield's street, she'd have gone every inch of the way.

Later that day, as we got off the school bus, Jeanine was reading my signup sheet. "I just want to see who's on it," she explained. "What are those hen scratchings?"

"Rooster scratchings," I corrected. "That's Jason's signature."

She studied it gravely for a minute. "Mary Frances, what do you think of Jason?"

Personally, I didn't think of him at all, if I could possibly help it, but I couldn't tell her that. "What do you mean?" I asked, carefully.

"Well —" She paused. "He doesn't seem very bright, sometimes. Oh, he knows football plays and baseball statistics and anything to do with sports, but that's all he ever talks about. It gets kind of boring after a while."

You could have knocked me over with a feather. Did that mean she was finally coming to her senses? "Maybe he just likes those things best," I suggested.

"Maybe." I could almost hear wheels churning around in my head. I mentally crossed my fingers. "Why, that's funny."

"What's funny?" I asked.

"Bruce Herrman's name isn't here."

With her thoughts so constantly on Jason Kirchfield, I wondered briefly why she was even concerned about Bruce. "He probably signed up in the office," I said.

"He didn't. I checked the list just before last period."

That made me wonder all the more. "He did just move here after all, Jeanine. I'm sure he could care less about the library."

"I guess." She frowned, as if trying to make up her mind about something. Then, suddenly, she blurted out, "Mary Frances, I have something to tell you."

From her pained expression, I knew I wasn't going to like whatever it was she was going to say. A picture came floating slowly out of my memory — a picture of Jeanine and Bruce on the dance floor, nestled cozily in each other's arms. Once Jeanine had said something about going after Bruce herself. Kiddingly, I'd thought at the time. Now she was apparently having doubts about Jason. And who could it be standing next in line? Bruce "Two r's" Herrman, that's who!

My little green devil was busily starting to weave knots in my stomach again. I didn't want to hear any more. I half turned, as if to leave.

"Bruce thinks you're stuck-up." Instantly, Jeanine clapped her hand over her mouth. "I didn't mean that, Mary Frances. Forget it." She walked away quickly.

The knots in my stomach unraveled for a minute, then just as fast, they rewound. I ran and caught up with Jeanine, grabbing the sleeve of her sweater. "Bruce Herrman thinks I'm a *snob?*" I yelled, partly from relief that Jeanine didn't have any designs on him, and partly because the very idea was so unbelievable. "Why I've hardly spoken to him!" I hadn't, either. In fact, I'd gone to a lot of trouble to avoid him. Every time he was around, it was nothing but disaster. I wanted him to like me. I couldn't deny that any longer. But did he really think I was a snob? I was determined to find out, although I didn't want Jeanine to know the real reason. "Who said so, anyway?" I demanded.

"Patti Hodgeson. Bruce told her that you never talk to him and whenever you see him, you find some excuse to take off. I didn't tell you before because I knew you'd be hurt."

"I'm not hurt," I lied, pushing my feelings down deep where they wouldn't show.

"Sure." I could tell she wasn't convinced.

"I have to get going, Jeanine," I said before she could add anything more. "It's my night to start supper."

I took all my feelings out on the carrots. Why, I asked myself as I scraped furiously, should what Bruce Herrman think make any difference to me? I could handle it. I was grown up, wasn't I? "Mature," I told the pile of carrot parings. "And mature people don't let little things get them down."

"She's talking to herself," said Matt as he and Mark strolled into the kitchen.

"Definitely the sign of a deranged mind," agreed Mark.

"Matt," I said, "did anybody ever tell you you were stuck-up?"

He reached out and swiped one of my carrots. "Never. You see here before you, little sister, the Universal Friend. Matt Courtney likes everybody and everybody likes Matt Courtney."

Mark snickered. "Except Cathy Purcell."

"Who's Cathy Purcell?"

"One of my conquests," said Matt.

"An ex-conquest," put in Mark. "She's the one we pulled the Switcheroo on last year, remember?"

The Switcheroo, as it was forever referred to, was when Matt and Mark changed dates one night, just to have some fun. Since even our family had trouble telling them apart sometimes, it had worked — for a while. Just when they thought they were safe, Matt made the mistake of bragging about it in public, and the story got back to his girl.

"But I won't rest until I've been granted a full pardon," Matt proclaimed now. "Cathy Purcell is one neat chick."

"Just like our Frankie here," Mark added. He grabbed a carrot, too, and started gnawing on it. "Who would ever think she was stuck-up?"

Who indeed?

Chapter 10

Ever since our big blow-up the day of the "Frankie" article, Angela hadn't been her old self. Maybe she was finished "emerging," or maybe I'd finally convinced her I didn't need two mothers. Whatever, she was a lot easier to live with.

Not that she'd actually apologized for what she'd said. That would have been like asking the ocean to dry up. She did, however, hang up my clothes a couple of times without giving me a big lecture on how she was tired of living in a pigsty and everything, although it was obviously difficult for her to keep her mouth shut sometimes. Once or twice I caught her biting her tongue nearly in half.

As for me, I was beginning to see that she hadn't been entirely wrong, either. After Jeanine had decided to start dressing up a bit, I'd been noticing other girls in school doing the same thing. Every day I was feeling more and more like an oddball, and no matter how often I told myself I didn't care, I did.

The morning following Jeanine's slip about Bruce Herrman's terrifically high opinion of me, I was taking one of my sweatshirts from my dresser. It was faded and there was a tiny rip on the neck — nothing too noticeable, but suddenly everything I owned looked shabby. I yanked out shirt after shirt, until they were all piled in the middle of the floor like a slightly used rainbow. I sat down on top of them and moaned. "For Pete's sake! Isn't there anything but junk around here?"

Fortunately, Angela had already left the room. I could just picture the smirk on her face.

It wouldn't have been so bad if this had been just an ordinary day. But last night, I'd decided that something was going to have to be done about Bruce Herrman. I couldn't let him go on forever thinking I was a snob when nothing was farther from the truth. I didn't expect him to fall all over me, of course. I wasn't, I reminded myself for the three thousandth time, "into" boys, as Jason Kirchfield would have put it. Still, my reputation mattered to me, and the sooner I straightened things out, the happier I was going to be.

I got to my feet and went over to the closet where Angela's wardrobe was hung neatly on hangers, slacks with slacks, blouses with blouses, and so on for about ten feet. I wondered how she ever made up her mind in the morning. There had to be something in there that would look better than my Salvation Army rejects.

At the back of the closet, apparently forgotten because she had nothing that matched it, was a soft, light green blouse of some kind of silky material. I slipped it off the hanger and held it up. The sleeves were a little dusty, but I could brush them off. I put it on, then looked in the mirror.

It was frillier than anything I'd ever worn, with dainty ruffles running down the front and around the collar. The color, though, seemed to bring out the coppery glints in my hair even more. I turned around slowly, admiring the effect. It would do, I told my reflection. I tucked it into the waistband of my jeans, then realized that the combination still didn't look quite right. The jeans were too casual. I grabbed a pair of gray slacks my mother had bought me a few months ago because she said she wanted me to have something decent, in case of an emergency. Well, if anything was an emergency, I thought, this was it. I pulled them on. The price tags were dangling from their plastic strings.

"Very nice," my mother remarked approvingly as I entered the kitchen a few minutes later.

"Thanks." I poured a glass of juice, made myself two pieces of buttered toast with strawberry jam and joined Kicky at the table. He was engrossed in a comic book. As I began eating, however, I could feel him eyeing me.

"What's wrong, Kick?" I asked.

"You look like somebody else again," he answered.

"Who?"

"I dunno. Miss Mosely, I guess. She's old, too."

My mother choked. I laughed and said, "Miss Mosely is your teacher, isn't she?"

"Yep. And you know what, Mary Frances? She told us all about that running thing for the library. Just like the one the paper said you were doing when they said your name was Frankie."

Kicky, with the elephant memory. "It's the same one," I told him. "Did you sign up?"

"Sure. I'm going to walk five miles. I want my movies back. They were going to show *Robin Hood*."

"That's the old Disney spirit. You might want to take my bedknob with you, though. That way, if you get tired, you can just wish yourself at the finish line."

"Aw, that's just a story," he scoffed. He must have had second thoughts, because after a couple of minutes he added, "Maybe I will anyway."

I finished my toast, grabbed my books and headed for the door.

"Good luck!" called my mother after me. She didn't say for what, but mothers are funny that way. It's probably ESP, but they seem to know when something big is happening.

I met Jeanine at the bus stop just as the bus was

rounding the corner. As soon as we were settled, she started in on a long involved discussion of some soap opera she'd been following. Compared to my life lately, the plot sounded about as complicated as Goldilocks and the Three Bears. I excused myself and went up the aisle to see if I could interest any more kids in signing up for the runathon. A lot of them already had, but I got two more signatures before we reached the school parking lot.

As we got off the bus, Dave Kruger, who sits next to me in English, snuggled up to me and whispered, "Hey, Frankie baby, want to run around with me?"

I still cringed slightly every time I heard that name, but then I remembered what my father had said, and smiled. "Sure. Right after you finish five miles for the library." I held out my signup sheet.

He staggered back, holding his stomach in agony. "What are you trying to do? Kill me?"

"You mean you can't run a measly five miles?" jeered one of his friends.

"You could always walk with the little kids," I suggested.

Blushing (it was kind of nice to see somebody else get the splotches for a change), he signed.

"I have to talk with Mr. Donnelly before math class," Jeanine remarked on the way into school. "I had trouble with one problem last night. I'll see you at lunch."

I was glad she had to leave. I'd already figured out that the best time to catch Bruce Herrman was before the bell rang. I was wondering how to do it without Jeanine finding out. I'd never hear the end of it.

I hung up my jacket and wandered over to where I knew Bruce's locker was. Kids milled around me as I stood there, fidgeting from one foot to the other and watching the hall clock creep slowly toward nine. There was no sign of Bruce. Had I missed him? I guess I was sort of hoping I had, when the hall cleared out and I spotted him walking toward me, his perfect nose leading the way. My hands began to get clammy and my knees were banging together like the cymbals in the school band.

He reached his locker without noticing me on the other side of the hall.

"Hi, Bruce," I said. My voice was shaking as bad as my knees.

"Huh?" He glanced up. "Oh, hi." He bent down and began to fiddle with the combination of his locker.

Short and sweet. I'd thoroughly rehearsed what I wanted to say the whole night before. At least I thought I had. But suddenly my mind went blank. I don't know why I was surprised. I should have expected it. I edged closer and tried again.

"Uh, I was wondering if you'd heard about the runathon we're having for the library."

He pulled out a book. "Sure."

"Well, I was wondering if you were planning to sign up."

"Why?"

That was one answer I hadn't anticipated. What could I say? That running was good for his physical development? That the library needed the money? Or the truth — that I liked him and wanted us to be friends?

"I don't know," I said miserably. "I just thought maybe you'd like to." I wished I had Kicky's magic bedknob so I could disappear. Timbuktu wasn't too far. "Actions speak louder than words," my father had told me. But right now words were what I needed. Why couldn't I think of the right ones?

"Look, Bruce," I tried again desperately, "I know I haven't exactly been very talkative lately. It — it's just that I've had a lot on my mind. I mean, the gum in my hair and working on this runathon thing and . . ." I trailed off, then took a deep breath. "The point is, I just don't want you to think North Valley is filled with idiots like me. It's really a nice place and I hope you're going to like being here." I turned away. I'd said everything I could think of to make him change his mind about me. If it hadn't worked, well, at least I'd tried.

Then I felt Bruce's hand touch my arm. I looked around, right into those gorgeous white, straight teeth. It was like being on a sunny beach in Florida.

"Thanks, Mary Frances," he said. "I guess maybe I've been trying too hard to fit in. I *do* like it here and I'm glad there's people like you and Jeanine and Jason. You've all helped make it a little easier. And I'll be glad to sign up for the runathon. Thanks for asking."

I couldn't believe my ears. "You will?"

"Sure. That's quite a project you're doing. I've been meaning to tell you."

"You have?"

"In fact, I know exactly how your little brother feels. I'm quite a movie fan myself."

"You are?"

He nodded. "When I was about five, they made a movie right in our city. My dad and I went down and got a chance to be extras. Ever since then, he says I've been star-struck."

"You did?" This was getting ridiculous. "What's your favorite?" I asked. "Movie, I mean."

"*Gone With the Wind.*"

"Hey, that's one of mine, too!"

"No kidding? I always liked the part where they burned down the city of Atlanta." With one smooth motion, he whipped my books from my arms and started down the hall. "You know, I've always wondered how they —"

The final bell brought me to my senses. "Bruce?"

"What?"

"My class is the other way."

He looked around, sort of dazed. Then he began to laugh and so did I.

It was funny, but my knees had suddenly stopped making music. It almost felt like we were back in the Castello, having a comfortable chat by the video game.

The only difference was that now I knew why Jeanine had acted like the Goodyear blimp. I couldn't explain it, but the same feeling was there.

He walked me right to Mrs. Novelli's science room, all the way explaining how he'd always wanted a moustache like Clark Gable's.

"You're going to be late for class," I reminded him, trying to picture him as Rhett Butler. Somehow he fit the part.

He handed back my books, leaned closer and growled in my ear. *"Frankie, my dear, I don't give a damn!"*

Chapter 11

The morning of the runathon, Angela came parading down the stairs wearing a powder blue jogging suit that looked like it was just off the Berkeley's Department Store rack, which, of course, it was. On her feet were matching powder blue sneakers. At the bottom of the steps, she spun around once, then struck a pose. "Well, how do you like it?"

"Gorgeous." It was, too. Sometimes I think Angela could wear a tent and still look stunning. "I didn't know you'd decided to run, though."

She came out of her pose. "And get all sweaty?" Some things never changed. "I *am* helping, though."

Angela had graciously agreed to sit at a table in front of the library and check the runners in. Even though it wasn't bringing in any money, I was glad she wanted to get involved. I didn't have to ask why, however. Paul Warnock had signed up to run.

The Apostles had offered to help, too. I gave them the job of standing along the sidelines with squirt bottles full of water, so anybody who got thirsty could have a drink. Just then, they were all out in the front yard acting like a bunch of crazy people, squirting each other and rolling all over the grass. As I glanced out the window, Matt wrestled Mark to the ground and poured a whole bottle over his head.

Kicky came out of the kitchen. "I'm all ready, Mary Frances," he said. He wasn't kidding, either. Starting at floor level, he had on: a pair of Mickey Mouse sneakers (naturally), red socks, green shorts, a yellow T-shirt, and, crowning his head, a ragged white sweatband that was eighty sizes too big and dropped down over his ears.

"Kick, you look really super," I told him, somehow with a straight face.

"Thanks. When are we leaving?"

"I have to go a little early. There's some stuff I have to take care of. You can go with Mom and Dad later."

Mr. Muldoon had called while I was eating breakfast.

"Good morning, young lady," he chirped. "What a glorious day you've ordered up." Well, of course I hadn't had anything to do with the weather, but it had turned out to be exactly the sort of day I could have asked for. The sky was bright blue, with marsh-mallowy puffs of clouds and a cool breeze keeping the temperature down.

"I was just wondering if you could arrive slightly ahead of schedule," Mr. Muldoon went on. "There are always some last-minute details that need supervising." We talked for a few minutes, then I hung up, promising to be at the library around nine o'clock.

I was waiting now for Jeanine, who'd said she'd go with me. She was supposed to have arrived five minutes ago. I was nervous enough without her being late. It kept going through my mind that maybe nobody would show up, and, if they did, maybe we wouldn't be able to earn enough money for the library. It would be terrible if after all the effort I'd put into it, Kicky still didn't get his movies. In fact, it would be worse than terrible. It would be a disaster, and I didn't think I could handle any more disasters in my life.

But eventually Jeanine showed up. "Hi," she said, opening the screen door. "Hurry up and get dressed. We've got to be there in five minutes."

"Jeanine, look at me. I *am* dressed."

"You're going in *that*?"

That was a pair of navy blue gym shorts with a white polo shirt over the top. Of course, next to Jeanine's pink and white satiny shorts and top, and her pink headband embroidered with roses, I guess I did look a little dull.

"This is it," I said. I held up one foot. "I did wash my sneakers, though, in case you didn't notice."

"Well, I just thought since you were going to be on television and all —" She trailed off.

"Jeanine, please don't bring that up. All night long all I kept dreaming about was thousands of eyes watching me. Right now, I just want to get there and get it over with, OK?"

"Relax. You'd think something terrible was going to happen." Later that night, I reminded her of that remark.

We left the house and walked downtown. All along the street, the police were setting up barricades and the traffic was edging past them slowly. The library building itself was decked out as if it was the Fourth of July. Red and white bunting was draped between the pillars and there were little American flags stuck into the stone flower pots in front. Mr. Muldoon and some of the library staff were setting up long tables on the sidewalk as Jeanine and I came up.

"Ah, there you are," said Mr. Muldoon, catching sight of us and smiling broadly. "And who is your charming friend who so much resembles a spring afternoon?"

"Jeanine's been helping me," I explained. I introduced them. Jeanine blushed prettily and shook Mr. Muldoon's hand.

"Yet another sterling example of young adulthood," he said. "Welcome." Jeanine looked at me.

"He thinks we're great," I translated.

"Oh."

"And now," Mr. Muldoon continued, "there are some people inside who would very much like to make your acquaintance."

It turned out to be the library's Board of Trustees — seven men and two women, all of them with vocabularies to match Mr. Muldoon's. Maybe when people work in a library, they just sort of absorb a bunch of words by osmosis. (I'd learned a *few* things from Mrs. Novelli.) I knew one or two of the trustees from seeing them around town. Each of them thanked me for what I was doing, which was nice of them. Jeanine stood back while all that was going on and once, when I glanced over, I thought she looked a little jealous. I'm not sure, but I may have grinned. I'm only human, after all.

When we went back outside, the street was filling up. Kids and parents were everywhere, like a parade was about to go marching by.

"There's the television crew," Jeanine hissed. She pointed to where a bunch of cables were strung along the pavement, resembling feeding time at the zoo's reptile house. "And there's Sally Winchester. I think she wants to interview you. She's coming this way."

"What? Oh, no!"

"Just act cool, Mary Frances. You can do it."

I was glad she had confidence in me. I wasn't so sure.

Sally Winchester, who was on the evening news, was a pretty girl, probably in her mid-twenties, but right then she looked like Dracula as she approached me, microphone in hand. She motioned to a man carrying a camera. I tried to grab Jeanine, but, friend that she is, she'd taken off somewhere, leaving me all alone.

"And this is —" Sally Winchester peered down at the pile of notes in her hand, "— young Frankie Courtney, who —"

"Mary Frances," I hissed.

"What?"

I cleared my throat. "My name is Mary Frances," I said again.

"Oh, well, we can cut that first part out. Jack!" She yelled at the cameraman. "Scratch that. We'll do a retake." She moistened her lips and faced the camera once more. "And here we have young Mary Frances Courtney, who came up with this marvelous idea to help out the library. How do you think it's going, Mary Frances?"

"Uh — good." I hadn't moved a muscle, yet sweat was pouring down my neck.

She gave a chuckle. "A woman of few words, I see. It says here that you hope to raise a thousand dollars.

That's a lot of money. Are you going to make your goal?"

I shrugged. What could I say? Her guess was as good as mine, and I wouldn't know the results until the next day, at least.

"I guess only time will tell, right?" I nodded. "Mary Frances, we wish you luck." She smiled into the camera. "This is Sally Winchester for WNVR News Today." She made a chopping motion to the guy named Jack. "That wasn't too bad, was it?" she said to me.

Not if you like turning into a nervous wreck in front of the entire population of North Valley. I don't think I'm cut out for television.

"Will all the participants please assume their positions," Mr. Muldoon's voice boomed over the loudspeaker. Nobody moved. Kids (and some parents) looked puzzled. "Uh, take your places," he said. Mr. Muldoon was learning.

Since our town was sort of small, a five-mile course would have ended up out in somebody's cow pasture, so Matt had suggested we set a one-mile course and everybody could do five laps. That way, he explained, the smaller children would be able to do their short walk and still end up back at the library.

As I went to the starting line, Jeanine materialized beside me. "Look at Jason, will you," she said. "He's trying to get on TV."

The WNVR crew was talking pictures of the crowd

and Jason Kirchfield was following their every move, smiling that stupid grin of his and sticking his chest into the camera, blotting everything else out of the picture.

"I don't know what I ever saw in him, Mary Frances," she confided. "He's so dumb, he's pathetic."

I wasn't going to hold my breath hoping she meant what she said. I needed it for running. But it was a definite sign of improvement.

"We'll be starting in about three minutes," came a different voice over the loudspeaker. "We'll start the runners first, then the smaller children, so they won't get trampled." He barked a laugh. Some of the little kids looked scared.

Mr. Muldoon came up to me carrying a small flag. On it someone had stitched John's design of the running book. "We'd like you to bear our standard, so to speak," he said placing it in my hand. "Just to start off. You may deposit it with one of the staff as soon as you wish."

I felt like one of those knights in a storybook, riding into battle with their lady's colors. I could have done without any more publicity, but if it would make Mr. Muldoon happy, it was the least I could do.

Someone was tugging at my sleeve. I turned around to find Bruce "Two r's" Herrman behind me. He was wearing an OKLAHOMA! sweatshirt.

"Miss Scarlett," he said with a Rhett Butler drawl,

"I'd be greatly honored if you'd let me run by your side."

"Why, fiddle-de-dee, Rhett," I flung back. "I don't know as I'd believe you could keep up with little ol' me." Out of the corner of my eye, I could see Jeanine's jaw drop down nearly to her pink sneakers.

"Mary Frances —" she began.

The gun went off.

Suddenly it was if I could run thirty miles, instead of just five. All this — everyone here — was because of me. Mary Frances Courtney. Across the way, my parents were smiling as if they'd just handed me the Nobel Prize. Next to me was Jeanine, who, no matter what, would always be my friend. And behind me, liking me for myself, was Bruce Herrman. I doubted I would ever feel so great again in my entire life.

Tears of happiness stinging my eyes, and the world in my pocket, I moved forward. I never saw the little boy with the ball standing on the curb. As the gun sounded, he jumped. The ball dropped to the ground and rolled into the middle of the street, coming to a stop right smack between my feet.

In that last split second, I had this crazy vision of a giant white sphere sailing through the air, four furry legs and a cat's tail — and *my* head — sticking out in all directions like quills on a porcupine. Then everything went blank as I hit the pavement.

Chapter 12

I don't remember too much of what happened next, but my father told me later that
it was like one of those old war movies where
the Marines are trying to capture some island. There's
a fierce battle, and when the first soldiers get shot,
their buddies grab the flag from their bloody hands
and charge on up the hill, more determined than ever.

"When you fell," my father said, "a couple of kids
landed on top of you. For a while, it was sheer pan-
demonium. Your mother and I rushed over, and so
did a lot of other people. Jeanine started to get hys-
terical. Mr. Muldoon kept wringing his hands and
looking like it was the end of the world. Nobody
seemed to know how to handle the situation. Than
some young kid saved the day."

"Who?" I asked.

"I didn't catch his name. Good-looking, with sort of sandy-colored hair?"

"Bruce Herrman," I breathed.

"Maybe. Anyway, I guess he realized that the best thing he could do was clear everyone out, so he picked up the little flag you'd been carrying and waved it in the air."

"He *did?*"

"Then he yelled, 'Let's finish this for Frankie!' or something like that, and that got everyone's attention. The kids all went on to finish their laps, while we brought you here."

"Here" was the hospital, where I lay with my leg encased in a huge cast that went all the way up to my hip. It wasn't a bad break, the doctor said, but he wanted me to stay overnight because of the lumps and bruises I got on my head when the kids fell on top of me.

That night, when the aches and pains had eased somewhat, I lay in my hospital bed, surrounded by flowers. Mr. Muldoon had sent over a beautiful arrangement of daisies, and the trustees gave me another one with fresh spring flowers. I looked like the Queen of the May, my mother said.

The Apostles had smuggled in a Castello's pizza — without mushrooms. Angela brought up her best bathrobe for me to wear, although she wouldn't let me put it on until I'd finished the pizza. Kicky had drawn a card with a bunch of scribbles and "Get Wele" written in kindergarten letters. Jeanine contented herself with calling me on the phone every half hour, wanting to know when I was coming home.

From Bruce, there was a single scarlet rose in a vase. The note said, "How's show biz — now that you're in the cast?" It was signed, "Rhett." Angela bugged me to tell her who it was from. I wouldn't.

Early the next morning, I got a call from Mr. Muldoon. He asked how I was feeling, then said, "From the tentative figures, we have been able to estimate that the runathon brought in about eighteen hundred dollars. Many of the children told me they'd gone an extra mile, just for you. And all your sponsors called to say that they would redeem your pledges at the full five-mile amount."

Eighteen hundred dollars! WOW! I couldn't have planned it better if I'd tried.

"So, we did more than break even," he went on, and I thought I heard him chuckle. I guess it was his way of making a joke.

Now Kicky and the other kids would have their movies, that much was certain, and I knew Mr. Muldoon would find something to do with the extra money.

Dr. Robertson, our family doctor, came in about ten o'clock and checked me over pretty carefully, especially my head. "I don't see anything here to cause you any trouble," he said when he was done. "On my way to work, though, I did see the Public Works truck in front of the library repairing a big hole in the street." I had to laugh, even though it gave me a headache. "I'll call your folks and tell them they can pick you up about noon."

I was glad to be going home. The food wasn't too bad, what I could eat of it on top of the pizza, but it wasn't like being with your own family. "I'm tired of lying here," I told Dr. Robertson. "Can't I have some crutches or something?"

He shook his head. "It's a bit early for that. I wouldn't have any objections to a wheelchair, though. Just stay away from the stairwells." He signed my cast (at least I think he did — it looked like a prescription) and left.

About a half hour later, the nurse brought the wheelchair, but I soon found out it's not as easy as it looks. After I'd edged past the door frame, trying to keep my leg from getting hung up, I took a couple of trips up and down the hall to get the feel of it. My arms soon got tired of doing the work my legs had always done, so I rested for a while in the visitors' area and read some magazines.

When I got bored with that, I headed back to my room to wait for my parents. I was beginning to get the hang of my new means of transportation, and as I neared my room, I glanced up and saw the corridor stretching out invitingly, with no one in sight except a man with a mop. I wondered what the wheelchair could really do. I mean, it *was* pretty tempting. A couple of good, hard pushes and I was flying along.

The oversized wheels covered ground quickly. Almost before I knew it, I was at the end of the corridor, with a wall directly in front of me. I tried to brake. My right hand gripped all right, but my left one kept slipping because it wasn't as strong. I took the corner on one wheel.

CRASH! I slammed into a hospital cart. Luckily, there was nobody on it.

The chair banged down and skidded to a halt. My heart was playing a drum solo in my chest.

Then I saw her. Flat against the wall, eyes open in terror, was a little old lady with silvery hair. She had both hands pressed against the front of her robe and she seemed to be gasping for breath.

A nurse came tearing out of a nearby room. "Mrs. Nottingham!" she cried. "Are you all right?"

The little old lady let out a deep, shuddering sigh and started fanning her face with a towel she had in her hand. "Yes, I think so," she said, haltingly. "Goodness, young lady, you really gave me quite a fright."

"Gosh, I'm awful sorry," I said, feeling almost like a murderer. The woman had practically had a heart attack. "I'm sorry," I repeated, but, I mean, really, what else could I say?

The nurse glared at me. "This is not the Grand Prix circuit, Miss Courtney. You could have caused an extremely serious incident."

"Now, now. Let the child be," Mrs. Nottingham

said, surprising both of us. "No harm done. Actually, I think I might have tried the same thing when I was younger."

After what I'd done, she sure was being awfully nice.

Suddenly, she peered into my face. "Why, you're the girl on television, aren't you?" she exclaimed. "I saw you last night on the news. A running thing for the library, wasn't it?"

I nodded.

"The library is one of my favorite places," she went on. "I go there quite often with my friends from the Senior Citizen Center to get books." She leaned closer and whispered, "I always enjoy watching the little children."

She sounded kind of sad and wistful when she said that. I wondered if she had any children of her own. If so, they must be all grown up by now. Maybe there were grandchildren.

"We'd better get you back to your room, Mrs. Nottingham," the nurse said briskly, taking the woman's arm. "Doctor will be coming soon with the results of your tests."

Mrs. Nottingham shook her arm free. "I'm perfectly capable of maneuvering on my own, thank you," she said with a trace of irritation. She smiled at me. "It was very nice meeting you." With that, she shuffled off slowly down the hall.

"I hope you're better soon," I called after her.

It was a full week before I could get back on my feet again. The cast had a little knob on the heel and they'd rented a pair of crutches for me to use. But being in a cast in July is like being in a torture chamber. The heat caused rashes where the plaster rubbed against my thigh and inside I itched so bad the Apostles took turns inventing gadgets so I could reach down and scratch.

Jeanine came over almost every day for that first week. I'd prop my leg up on the couch and we'd watch soap operas for hours. Actually, that made me look at things a little differently when I saw what those characters had to go through — week after week, year after year. And I thought *I'd* had troubles!

One night, after I'd managed to start moving around a bit on my crutches, Bruce Herrman called and told me they were showing *Gone With the Wind* on cable.

"Why don't you come over here and we'll watch it together?" I said, surprising myself with my coolness.

"Hey, thanks! I'll be there around eight," he said.

By the time he got there, though, I felt itchy all over, and not just my leg. I mean, it was nice having someone be interested in the same things I was, but there was the danger of Angela making a big thing out of me entertaining a boy. With any luck, she'd be going out with her friends and wouldn't even know about it. But then, I'd learned luck was a funny thing. Sometimes you had it, and sometimes you didn't.

This time I didn't. Angela didn't have a thing to do except sit in the living room and pretend to be absolutely *enthralled* with the costumes and scenery of the Old South. Her eyes, however, kept switching back and forth from the television to Bruce to me.

"Don't you have cable?" she asked while Scarlett was following Ashley Wilkes around like a puppy dog.

"TV's broken," Bruce answered.

Was that why he'd called? Because his television was on the blink? *Boys,* I told myself furiously. I'd been right not wanting to get mixed up with them. For a while I'd decided there really wasn't anything wrong with liking somebody. But I guess I'd gone too far. I was acting just like Jeanine and Angela. I sat there, angry at myself, and wondering if I was going to have to find some other project to occupy my mind.

By the time they got to the burning of Atlanta, Angela was bored and took off to her room, leaving Bruce and me in peace and quiet. As I watched the flames sweep over the city, Bruce turned to me.

"I was just kidding about our TV," he said. "I have an older sister and she's just as big a pest."

My head started spinning. Was I ever going to get things straightened out?

For the last half hour, Bruce turned down the sound and imitated all the voices. He's pretty good at mimicking Clark Gable, although I still would have liked to have seen him with a moustache. The whole thing was so confusing.

"I'll think about it tomorrow," I said silently along with Scarlett.

My leg stayed in the cast for four weeks, then I had to go back to the hospital and have it sawed off — the cast, not my leg, although it felt just as scary. Underneath, my skin was all dry and scaly and pale. My other leg was tan, so they looked really weird next to each other. I still needed the crutches for a little while, though.

Mr. Muldoon had called while I was at the hospital and had left a message that he'd like me to come to the library as soon as I felt up to it. Well, I was pretty fast on the crutches by then, so I scooted myself down the eight blocks to downtown, holding my leg out as much as possible so the sun could get to it.

Mr. Muldoon was standing in the lobby and his face lit up when I hopped in.

"You've misplaced your cast," he said.

"Just this morning," I said.

"Excellent. The reason I called was that we've just completed a new display and I'd like your opinion of it."

What was I, the new director of public relations?

But I let him lead the way into the main reading room and over to the bulletin board where the public announcements were pinned up.

The center of the bulletin board had been cleared

away and in big, black cutout letters were the words, COMING ATTRACTIONS. Beneath it was a poster of Donald Duck, with a notice that a new Walt Disney movie series would be starting in the fall.

Next to it, where nobody could miss it, was a photo of a young girl with short, carrot-colored curls. It had a caption, too.

"In Grateful Appreciation of Mary Frances Courtney, Who Gave of Herself so That Others Could Have."

My eyes grew misty. "You didn't have to do that," I said, huskily.

"Ah, but I did, you know," answered Mr. Muldoon.

I couldn't even get out "Thanks," but I think he knew I wanted to.

On the way out, I glanced over at the Children's Department. "What's that?" I asked Mr. Muldoon.

"Something else I wanted to show you," he replied.

What I'd noticed was two huge wooden rocking chairs. In one sat a gray-haired woman, and on her lap was a tiny boy. They were both engrossed in a picture book. It was hard to tell who was having a better time.

"A friend of yours stopped in last week," Mr. Muldoon continued. "A Mrs. Nottingham."

"From the hospital," I breathed.

"From the Senior Citizen group, she said," he corrected. "She told me about meeting you and how impressed she was about what you'd accomplished for the library. She informed me that she'd discussed it with a group of her friends. They decided that since youngsters could come up with such outstanding projects, the older members of our community could do the same. They thought up this idea. They're calling it 'Rocking Chair Reading Hours' and many of our senior citizens have volunteered to come in weekly and read to the little ones. I could think of no better use for the extra money earned in the runathon than to provide the only other necessity. The rocking chairs."

Summer is almost over. My leg is now nearly back to normal — good enough, at least, for a couple of quick shopping trips with Jeanine to pick out new clothes for starting ninth grade, and a few other adventures. No jeans and no sweatshirts, though. My father groaned a bit when he got the bills, but then I pointed out how much I'd been saving him over the past few years by not accumulating my own department store like Angela had.

"I mean, I *am* growing up," I said.

"Correction. You *are* grown up," he replied. "I was just making fatherly noises. I'm a very lucky man to be able to call you my daughter."

I grinned — from pierced ear to pierced ear.

Last night Jeanine called me on the phone. "His name is Mike," she bubbled. "He's into computers and all sorts of electronic stuff. He says he's going to teach me about them. Won't it be *great?* He wants to meet me at the Castello tonight, Mary Frances. I can't go alone. Please? Will you come with me?"

I wonder if somebody out there is making another snowball.